# MATRONS OF DISHONOUR

*Esther & Jack Enright Mystery*
*Book Thirteen*

**David Field**

*Also in the Esther & Jack Enright Mystery Series*

The Gaslight Stalker

The Night Caller

The Prodigal Sister

The Slum Reaper

The Posing Playwright

The Mercy Killings

The Jubilee Plot

The Lost Boys

The Retirement Murders

The Long Delayed Revenge

The Belvedere Scandal

The Footlights Murder

# MATRONS OF DISHONOUR

Published by Sapere Books.

24 Trafalgar Road, Ilkley, LS29 8HH

saperebooks.com



ISBN: 978-0-85495-862-7

# CHAPTER ONE

*Hertfordshire, 1909*

Esther Enright sighed with irritation when she saw Doris Walker waiting politely in the open doorway of her senior classroom while she was wiping the blackboard clean at the end of the day's classes. The nine children in Esther's class had long since departed, as had the twenty or so in Doris's combined Primary One and Two class, and Esther had been promising herself an early return home. However, Doris was a most efficient teacher, if somewhat lacking in initiative, and as headmistress and proprietor of Cassiobury House Private School in Watford, it behoved Esther to at least listen to what Doris apparently needed to impart.

She smiled as she collected her chalks and placed them in the drawer of her desk, then walked over to where Doris was waiting with her usual deferential, and somewhat apologetic, half smile. 'How were today's classes?' she asked by way of an ice-breaker.

'They went very well,' Doris replied, 'particularly the introduction to long division, which most of the class seemed to grasp without difficulty. However, I'm a little concerned about Clarissa Melrose. She used to be so lively, and was one of the first to contribute to class discussion. But lately she seems to have withdrawn, and I can't get her to talk.'

'These things happen, of course,' Esther reminded her. 'It may be that there's some temporary difficulty at home, and we just have to probe gently in order to discover what it is.'

'I've tried that,' Doris explained, 'but she just withdraws even further inside her own little shell. I was wondering if you might have a word with her, since you'll know more about the family.'

Esther had made it her business to learn as much as she could about the backgrounds of those children whose comfortably off parents sent their children to Cassiobury House. This had been the policy of her mentor, friend, patron and benefactor Emily Allsop, who some years ago had purchased the school when it had been in decline due to poor management and indifferent proprietorship. Emily had appointed Esther as her Deputy Headmistress when she'd recognised her innate talents during the teacher training that she'd then been supervising. Esther had happily accepted the post, moving her entire family from London to Watford so that she could be within walking distance of the school. They still lived at The Lodge, which was on the northern boundary of Cassiobury Park. When Emily had died of consumption four years previously, with no close relatives, she'd left the school to a stunned and eternally grateful Esther, who'd made it her life's mission to continue the good work that Emily had begun, and in doing so honour her memory.

Getting to know the families whose fees were the school's lifeblood had been one of the first policies that Emily had insisted on. Esther knew that Clarissa's father was a successful dentist with rooms in Market Street, in the centre of Watford. She'd first met James Melrose and his wife Antonia when they'd enquired into the possibility of entrusting the school with the education of their only child Clarissa, who had thrived in the two years since she'd joined Primary One. At seven years old, Clarissa was usually lively and had several friends. It was unlike her to be so subdued, and Esther knew of nothing that could account for it, except perhaps a downturn in her father's dental practice, and the possibility that there would be no spare money for future school fees.

'I'll make a point of speaking with Clarissa tomorrow, perhaps during the lunchbreak,' Esther offered.

Doris nodded. 'I'd be very much obliged if you would, although she's still here, if you think that this might be a better opportunity.'

'Still here?' Esther echoed. 'Surely the children left a quarter of an hour ago?'

'The rest of them, certainly,' Doris confirmed, 'but Clarissa seemed to hang back. Part of her current malady seems to be a reluctance to mix with her classmates. When I last saw her, just before coming to you, she was sitting on the stump of that old beech tree that you had cut down because it was becoming dangerous for the children to play on.'

'Very well. Thank you, Doris,' Esther replied. 'I'll go and see if I can get to the bottom of this.'

The two women left by way of the front door, and Esther glanced across to where a sad-looking Clarissa Melrose was still seated on the old tree stump, head down. Esther walked over and tried to keep it light-hearted.

'I'm glad we found a use for this old stump,' she began, 'but shouldn't you be making your way home along with the others?'

Clarissa shrugged but remained silent, so Esther tried another approach.

'Won't your mother be anxious when you're home late? And don't Mary Jolley and Mabel Rogers live on the same street as you? Don't you normally walk home with them?'

'They don't want to be with me now, because I'm always sad,' Clarissa admitted.

This was a valuable opening, and Esther opted to take it. 'Why are you sad, Clarissa? And if your mother sees Mary and Mabel walking home without you in their company, won't she worry what's happened to you?'

'Mama's in hospital,' Clarissa all but whispered, 'and the only one who'll notice me being late home is old Sarah, the housekeeper. Papa doesn't close his practice for the day until after five o'clock, so he won't be home to notice.'

Sensing that they'd reached the core of the girl's melancholy, Esther gently probed a little further. 'Is your mother likely to be in hospital for a good deal longer?'

'Perhaps forever,' Clarissa muttered. 'She's been there since last October, and Christmas in our house was truly *dreadful*.'

'She must be very ill,' Esther replied with genuine sympathy.

'The doctors don't seem to know. It's inside her body, they say. Something got "ruptured" — is that the right word?'

'Yes, it is,' Esther assured her, 'but how did it happen? Did she have a fall or something?'

'She was hit in the stomach by a big bully police constable with a big stick,' Clarissa told her as her face began to crumple.

Esther put her arm around the girl's shoulders. 'That's *awful*, Clarissa. My husband's a police officer, as you may know, and he'd never do that to a woman.'

'This one did,' Clarissa went on as a tear rolled down her cheek. 'And Mama was only just standing there, at a meeting with other ladies.'

'Where was this?' Esther asked. 'Surely not here in Watford?'

'No,' said Clarissa with a shake of her auburn braids, 'this was somewhere in the middle of London. Near Parliament, I think. Mama wasn't the only one, and it was weeks before we could see her. She's still in the same hospital, near London Bridge, and we can only get in to visit her at weekends.'

'What was your mother doing when she was beaten by the police officer?'

'Just standing at a meeting with lots of other ladies. Something to do with a change in the law that they wanted to see. Papa says it was all a load of nonsense, and Mama should have known better than to be there. But she wasn't the only one — there were hundreds more, it seems, and Mama was one of the unlucky ones, standing near the front when all these policemen charged at them. Quite a few of them were arrested, and Mama wasn't the only one taken to hospital, or so Papa says.'

'And that's why you've been so sad and withdrawn lately?' Esther asked.

Clarissa nodded. 'Can you imagine *your* life without a mama?'

'I don't have to,' Esther confided, 'since I lost *both* my parents in a riverboat tragedy on the Thames when I was fifteen. I would have been put in an orphanage, had it not been for a kindly old friend of the family who took me in. But it wasn't the same without my own mother, so I know how it must be for you.'

'I wish my school friends did,' Clarissa said with a sigh. 'Most of them say that they'd rather be without their mothers, because then they'd be free to do what they like. But it's not like that when it actually happens.'

'Indeed not,' Esther agreed. 'Anyway, if you need someone to talk to in the future, you can always come to me. Teachers are like second mothers, in some ways.'

'But you've already got your own children, my friends tell me,' said Clarissa. 'And they went to this school, didn't they?'

'My girls, certainly, and we adopted another who was a student at this school. But I can always make time to talk with you, whenever you wish.'

'That's very kind of you, Mrs Enright,' Clarissa replied, finally smiling. 'Now I suppose I'd better go home, or the housekeeper will report me to Papa, and he'll want to know what I've been up to.'

Esther watched as Clarissa made her way through the school gates, clearly in no hurry to return to what must be a sad household, and her heart went out to her. Esther herself had so much to thank God for in her life, with a loving husband and five children — four natural, one adopted. Determined to learn how a respectable, middle-class wife of a professional man had come to be beaten by a police officer, she made her way home, deep in thought. Her husband, Jack Enright, was head of Recruitment and Manpower at Scotland Yard, and he'd spent many years as an active police officer prior to that. Perhaps he'd have some answers.

'I don't know how it happened, do I?' Jack protested once Esther had told him Clarissa's story. 'I don't have anything to do with actual street operations.'

'But you could find out, surely?' Esther persisted. 'I was horrified to learn that the mother of one of my own pupils was hurt badly enough to be hospitalised. That was last October, and it's now February, so her injuries must be very serious.'

'It sounds as if she was one of those "Votes for Women" troublemakers,' Jack replied. 'According to the papers, they've become less law-abiding as time has gone on.'

'I've long since learned not to believe everything I read in the newspapers,' Esther said dismissively, 'which is why I'm so alarmed by Annabelle's determination to become one of those reformists who only get half the facts right, then publish the *other* half.'

Annabelle was the Enrights' adopted daughter who'd become part of the family after her father had murdered her mother and been hanged for it, making Annabelle an orphan. She'd also been one of Esther's pupils at Cassiobury House School. Esther and Jack had provided her with a home during term time, while Jack's ageing aunt and uncle, Percy and Beatrice Enright, invited her to stay at their house in Hackney during the school holidays. She'd more than rewarded their kindness and faith in her, and now, at nineteen — the same age as Esther and Jack's eldest child, Lillian — she was seeking an outlet for her passion for writing.

Her room was full of half-written stories, plays and poems, and she was an avid reader of novels and newspapers. Slowly, under the influence of what she was reading daily, she'd formed an ambition to join the ranks of those who supplied the public with their daily dose of news, but had learned to her chagrin that it remained one of the many professions from which women were excluded by means of a tacit conspiracy among male newspaper proprietors and editors.

'Those reformist crusaders about whom you complain certainly have enough to get their teeth into,' said Jack. 'Dreadful housing conditions in the poorer working-class areas, high infant death rate, diseases rampant because of unsanitary conditions, corruption within those areas of government that ought to be fixing these problems, the constant demands of the Irish for independence, and of course that strident mob that your pupil's mother was probably involved with, asking for the impossible. You know, that crowd of agitators that you were once part of?'

'I was *never* a part of them,' Esther snapped. 'If you recall, I pretended to go along with them and joined the outer fringes at Uncle Percy's request, as part of that awful murder investigation. That was at least four years ago, and I haven't been near them since. Anyway, lately they seem to have been confronting police officers. That's why I believe you can find out why Antonia Melrose was so badly hurt.'

'I can try,' Jack said with a shrug. 'But you might not like what I find out.'

'I'll take that risk. I just think that it's awful that a respectable woman who did nothing worse that attend a public meeting could end up being brutalised by some hulking bobby armed with a billy club. Aren't they supposed to *protect* those weaker than themselves?'

'From what I've read, some of those "respectable women" have taken to hurling rocks at bobbies, and rolling marbles under the hooves of police horses in the hope of unseating their riders,' said Jack.

'Just find out what happened, that's all I'm asking,' Esther repeated. 'When we know the facts, we can start to make moral judgments. And I repeat — don't base your opinions solely on what you read in the newspapers.'

The following morning, Jack sighed as he opened the file that his assistant, Sergeant Copley, had brought him from Records. He had quite enough to occupy his brain at work without worrying about developments at home.

At Scotland Yard there was a push for higher levels of recruitment, and given Jack's position as Chief Inspector in charge of Recruitment and Manpower, the main burden of that fell on him. Recent public disorders had thinned the uniformed ranks, both by reason of the number of street bobbies hospitalised after riots, and the resignations that had occurred in the wake of family men being persuaded by their wives to give up a profession in which they could get killed or seriously maimed. The serving numbers were down by a significant percentage, and Jack was conducting recruitment interviews daily in an attempt to restore them.

But this problem almost paled into insignificance when his troubled mind returned to his ongoing concern for his eldest son, Bertie, now seventeen years old and seemingly determined to die a military hero. For as long as he'd been able to think for himself, Bertie had been obsessed with the army, and had progressed from playing with toy soldiers to building forts in which to house them, then haunting bookshops for written accounts of ancient battles. At the age of seven, he'd been recruited into something called the 'Boys' Battalion', which was sponsored by their Watford neighbour, the Earl of Essex. He owned Cassiobury Park, which lay immediately behind the family home.

The earl was a major in the Hertfordshire Yeomanry, a volunteer force that had, as a result of significant reforms the previous year, become recognised as part of a new volunteer component of the British Army. This had been intended to supplement the regular army, but, following vigorous political opposition, it had been limited to home defence. This meant that those within its ranks could be called into service anywhere within the country, but could not be compelled to serve overseas. However, Jack was cynical enough to be fearful that such an arrangement could be reversed with a single stroke of a pen at the War Office, and conflict with Germany under its bellicose Kaiser Wilhelm was becoming more likely by the month.

The earl made no secret of the fact that he was committed to recruiting promising boys into his regiment, and the Boys' Battalion had been formed from those sturdy youths who might be found taking exercise and playing games on the earl's land. Despite Jack's best efforts, Bertie had become an eager recruit and had found favour with the earl, who saw officer potential in the keen young man. To keep him well motivated, the earl had ensured that Bertie was one of the first to be elevated to junior officer status. As a second lieutenant at the ridiculously young age of seventeen, he was never happier than when he was parading up and down, sometimes even in the house, in his immaculate uniform with its always glistening cap badge. Sighing, Jack consoled himself with the thought that at least his youngest children, Miriam and Thomas, weren't currently giving him any cause for worry. He just had to hope that Thomas didn't develop a similar obsession with the military as he grew older.

Jack forced his thoughts back to the open file on his desk, and read with mounting concern about the dreadful event that it recorded. Since 1903, an organisation known as the Women's Social and Political Union (referred to as the WSPU for short) had been campaigning for a more equal role in the nation's affairs for women, with the ultimate goal of being allowed to vote in national elections and to stand for Parliament themselves. Its progenitors were a mother and two daughters from Manchester, the Pankhursts, and they'd been steadily gathering supporters. They could now boast many thousands of likeminded women who were no longer content with the humble, servile role they'd been assigned in society. They'd petitioned, buttonholed politicians, and engaged in loud protest marches, waving banners that were emblazoned with their demand: *Votes for Women.*

Three years ago, a journalist had given them the name by which they were now generally known, the Suffragettes, and they'd begun to resemble an army. Their marching tune was an adaptation of the revolutionary French battle melody 'La

Marseillaise', while their chosen colours were purple, green and white, which were used on banners, ribbons, hats and sashes. They had also raised the level of violence employed on their protest marches — whether this was of their own accord, or in response to increased violence from the police lines with which they regularly clashed, was a matter for conjecture.

On the thirteenth of October the previous year, Emmeline Pankhurst, the matriarch, and her equally determined daughter Christabel, had organised what they euphemistically called 'a rush' on the House of Commons, intent on presenting a petition to Prime Minister Asquith. They'd managed to recruit sixty thousand to their banners, and they seriously outnumbered the five thousand police officers who were waiting for them. In the aftermath of the bloody melee that followed, without a single Suffragist making it through the doors of Parliament House, there had been thirty-seven arrests and ten hospitalisations.

This much had been coldly reported in the newspapers, but as Jack read the details in the reports from officers who had actually been there, the full trauma emerged from phrases like 'beaten over the head by a woman armed with a length of wood that was surmounted with the usual placard, but had nails protruding from its entire length', and 'Constable Purvis fell from his mount, and was dragged out from under it by three determined women who then set about kicking him in the testicles.'

There was little to report from the other side of this contest, as was to be expected, but Jack could well understand the naked fear that had caused both front lines to react so brutally. He searched in vain for the name he was seeking, but perhaps she was the one referred to in a report concerning 'a lady, later learned to have travelled all the way from Watford, who was dragged away screaming in pain, and on the advice of Police Surgeon Bebbington was taken down to Guy's Hospital in a paddy wagon.'

'It seems that Antonia Melrose was in the front line, where much of the violence occurred,' Jack reported back to Esther that evening. 'Do you expect men with wives and families to just stand there and allow themselves to be attacked with lengths of wood studded with nails, or kicked in the privates? How would *you* feel if I was rostered onto duties like that? No wonder so many police wives are persuading their men to quit the force, which is making my job impossible.'

'All I know is that there's a seven-year-old girl missing her mother because some brute in a uniform took it upon himself to beat her with a billy club,' Esther retorted. 'How do you justify that?'

'I don't, and I can't. I'm just saying that none of that would have happened if there hadn't been a forced march on the House, with the aim of overrunning its security.'

'They were respectable middle-class ladies determined to make their point to our nation's rulers.'

'They were armed with weapons, and determined to slug it out with bobbies,' Jack insisted.

Esther gave a snort of frustration as she turned and walked towards the living room door. 'We seem to be as divided as the nation is over the right of women to have a say in how our country is run,' she observed. 'It's lamb chops for supper, so let's leave it at that and enjoy Polly's cooking.'

# CHAPTER TWO

Percy Enright had just finished planting the seeds of his next crop of runner beans in the extensive vegetable garden to the rear of his home in Victoria Road, Hackney. As he stretched back upright, two sensations reminded him that he was well into his seventies. The first was his shortage of breath after having spent several minutes bent double over his paunch — the visible legacy of a lifetime's devotion to food. The second was the twinge that began above his buttock and ran down his left leg. The doctor had given it some fancy Latin name, and had prescribed tablets that would have been equally effective had Percy fed them to next door's cat. But he was not one for giving in to minor discomforts, else he would not have led the life he had.

In his younger years he'd slogged it out with the best of them while sporting the uniform of first a police constable, then a sergeant, before someone in the Metropolitan Police had found a better use for his enquiring mind and his talent for devious avoidance of the procedures manual that normally governed police enquiries. He'd retired twelve years ago at the rank of Detective Inspector, leaving behind him a legend that spoke of many collars felt, many rules bent to the point of fracture, and a healthy disrespect for authority. His still lively brain had refused to retire with him, however, and for almost a decade he'd pursued a second career as a confidential enquiry agent. His services had been in high demand, and not always from private clients. There were still those in the Government who occasionally required the skills of a man who knew how to operate under a false identity or a cunning disguise in order to unofficially conduct slightly murkier enquiries.

But even that had bored Percy after a while, so he'd sold his business for an outrageously optimistic sum and finally retired to his vegetable patch, whose greatest attraction was its distance from his house, where his long-suffering, but not silently suffering, wife Beattie ruled with an eagle eye and a razor-sharp tongue.

However, old habits die hard, and as he caught the muffled sound of a coach trundling slowly down Victoria Road, his experience told him that it was a large one, and therefore probably of official origin, and that its coachman was searching for a certain house number. He heard the coach stop outside what was probably his front gate, and as he pretended to lean forward in order to pick up his empty seed tray, he looked surreptitiously towards the front hedge at the end of the path that led down the side of the house. The Derby hat that was visible as its wearer peered through the gaps in the privet confirmed his initial suspicion. He was therefore fully prepared when a tall, fashionably dressed man appeared at the top of the path and began to walk slowly towards him.

'Mr Enright?' the man asked.

Percy smiled dismissively. 'You obviously already knew that, so don't mess me about. Is it Melville or Kell?'

'I beg your pardon?'

Percy gave one of his loud, dramatic sighs. 'I've just finished planting some runner beans, and they're likely to reach full maturity before you give me a straight answer, so I'll tell you what I've already deduced, shall I? Neither my bookmaker nor my dentist is in the habit of sending a coach for my convenience, and your driver was clearly looking for the address he'd been given. The last time I was collected by coach was in order to be transported to a certain secret house on Tufnell Park Road, and on that occasion it collected me outside my former business premises. That was four years ago, and I assume that a certain Government department of whose existence not even the Government is aware requires my services, for reasons that I cannot fathom. So I ask again: were you sent by Vernon Kell, or — God forbid — William Melville?'

'I'm not at liberty to say, sir.'

'But since you're dressed like an undertaker on his day off, may I take it that you work for MO3?'

'No, sir — MO5.'

'I'll refrain from enquiring what happened to "MO4" in the interim, and ask if my proposed journey is in any way optional.'

'It is not, sir. But how were you able to anticipate all this?'

'Bitter experience, and the sort of analytical brain that is clearly about to be employed in something covert and potentially embarrassing to those who pay your annual salary. May I advise my wife of my imminent departure?'

'The fact of it, certainly, sir, but not the precise destination.'

'Very well, allow me a few moments to change out of my gardening clothes, and to advise her that there will be one less victim for today's threatened lunch. I'll emerge from my front door in due course, thereby obviating any need on your part to engage that pistol you've made such a poor job of concealing inside your cutaway jacket. I recommend a fuller style if you wish to maintain an innocuous appearance.'

'I was told you were tricky,' the man replied with a grin.

'By Melville?'

'Yes, sir.'

'See?' Percy said triumphantly. 'It took me a full five minutes to prise from you the answer to my original question, but we got there in the end. Go round to the front and admire my rose bushes while I get changed.'

Percy found Beattie in their sitting room, reading the latest newsletter from the Methodist Mission that enjoyed her lifelong patronage.

'I have to go out,' he told her, 'and I probably won't be home for lunch, if Dame Fortune smiles upon me and I'm supplied with an edible alternative.'

'In that coach that pulled up outside the door?' she asked.

'They don't serve lunch inside that, but I imagine that they will when I reach my destination.'

'Don't go missing for days, like you used to,' she instructed him sternly.

He shook his head. 'That is *very much* in the past, I hope, but expect me when you see me.'

'My God, you're looking old,' William Melville gloated as he looked up from behind the desk in the office into which Percy had just been ushered.

'And you look as if you died two years ago,' Percy muttered back. 'When did MO3 become MO5? Is that a promotion, or just an attempt to mislead a Government that finally learned that it was paying for MO3?'

'You don't need the details, Percy, but you should be advised that around here I'm now known simply as "M".'

'Short for "moron"?'

'Ever the diplomat,' Melville replied sourly. 'I suppose you came here in expectation of Victoria sponge cake?'

'I came here in your coach, which was far more comfortable than the horse bus you used to employ. As for my dietary requirements, it must be almost lunchtime, and I recommend the beef roast that I smelled on my way in.'

'It's actually lamb,' Melville told him. 'I hope that your powers of investigation haven't gone as far south as your sense of smell.'

'Do I get my instructions before or after the lamb?'

'During, I thought.'

'Will we be joined by Kell?'

'Perhaps. He's currently with the Secretary of State for War — a chap called Haldane, who's decided to set up yet another covert department that Vernon will be heading up, probably with me as his deputy. But I have full authorisation to brief you on your latest project.'

'One to which I haven't yet consented, or is that formality already dispensed with?' Percy demanded.

'You knew the score when you opted to step inside my coach, Percy, so let's not pussyfoot around,' Melville retorted.

'I "opted", as you call it, to enter your coach because the alternative was being shot in my own vegetable garden,' Percy said with a glower. 'Given that I'd just planted next season's runner beans, it seemed appropriate to remain alive to see them mature. So what is it this time? Another royal scandal? A peccadillo by a Cabinet minister? An East End tottie threatening to expose her night on the tiles with the Archbishop of Canterbury?'

'Don't you want to wait until lunchtime?'

Percy took out his fob watch and pretended to consult it. 'This watch tells me that it wants half an hour, as no doubt does the roast, but my stomach tells me that it's time to eat, so how about we while away the time by drinking whisky and soda?'

An hour and a half later, the two of them were still the only ones around the lunch table, and Percy had consumed half a leg of lamb.

'What do you know about a group of ladies — and I use that term entirely genetically — who call themselves the "Amazons"?' Melville asked.

'A group of Greek women who, in their enthusiasm to be warriors, went so far as to cut off one breast so that their skills with a bow and arrow would not be impeded?'

'Purely a myth, or so I'm led to understand,' Melville replied. 'The ones to whom I refer are believed to be here in London, and part of that "Votes for Women" mob, to whom they're less romantically known as "The Bodyguard". '

'And this is of interest to me why, exactly?'

'Because I want you to track them down, identify them, and have them lined up for a buckling.'

'No great stretch there, then,' Percy replied sarcastically. 'Is there a pudding to follow this excellent main course?'

'Only if you shut up and listen, you incorrigible gannet,' Melville said with a frown. 'Now, I assume that you won't need to take notes, but if you do we'll take them off you before you leave, so listen *very* carefully.'

'At least it seems that I'll be allowed to leave eventually, so fire away,' Percy invited him.

Melville instinctively lowered his voice. 'Just over a week ago, there was an armed robbery on the premises of Brunner Mond, who occupy factory premises in Silvertown, which you may know from your East End days. If not, it's located on the north bank of the Thames, and it's an industrial complex accessed by way of Woolwich Road, between the entrances to the Victoria and Royal Albert Docks. The outrage was committed at two in the morning, and the robbers got away with a wagonload of the firm's current main product. It's called "trinitrotoluene" by industrial chemists, but is more commonly known as "TNT", and is highly explosive.'

'We must be closer to war than the public are being led to believe,' Percy observed. 'May I assume that it was being manufactured under Government licence, and that its loss will prove to be highly embarrassing to said Government?'

'Even more embarrassing than you might think. You're correct, of course, and we are currently anticipating a need for a vast increase in the shells we have available to hurl at an enemy that must remain undisclosed, but will no doubt turn out to be Germany. The TNT is apparently to be combined with something called ammonium nitrate, and we need a huge supply of it.'

'I have a feeling that there's more to come, and that this will prove to have been something other than your routine robbery, given the nature of the loot,' Percy prompted.

'In view of the sensitive, not to mention dangerous, nature of the product, the firm employed not just a group of nightwatchmen, but also several uniformed officers from the Met. On the night in question, a total of five suitably armed men were overrun by a group of women.'

Percy suppressed a laugh and asked, 'Those "Amazons" to whom you referred earlier?'

'Precisely,' Melville confirmed. 'Ten of them, by all accounts, armed with wooden clubs that they produced from under their voluminous skirts at the very last moment. They took the guard by surprise, clearly, which explains why four of them were knocked out cold, while the fifth took to his heels.'

'And to what purpose do we believe that this TNT will be put?' Percy asked as he kept his face straight.

'The purpose for which it was intended,' Melville answered gravely. 'Explosions.'

'This "Votes for Women" lot have previously only hit out at bobbies on line restraint duties,' Percy reminded him. 'What makes you think that they're planning to shell the House?'

'Clearly, they aren't into shell manufacture — at least, not yet — but their activities have recently extended to acts of malicious damage,' Melville explained. 'Smashed windows, in the main, but on at least one occasion they set fire to a letterbox. The fear is that the explosives are destined for the houses of those leading Cabinet members who are perceived, rightly or wrongly, to be opposed to female suffrage.'

'This has clearly not been made public because of the fear of mass panic,' Percy observed, 'but have the Cabinet members themselves been told of the potential danger?'

'Of course, and we've doubled the normal level of security that we extend to them. But that's not why you've been called in.'

'I was wondering when we'd get to that,' Percy said with a smile, 'so now I presumably learn what song I have to sing for my supper?'

'I think I already mentioned that, Percy. I want these women found, charged and taken out of circulation.'

'By me? Why not let the local bobbies do their work? I'm out of touch these days, I know, but in my time the men in Whitechapel knew the docks area like their own living rooms.'

'There's obviously a need for secrecy, for several reasons,' Melville told him.

'The obvious one being the fact that you don't want the spies who work for Germany — and don't try to deny their existence — to know about what was being manufactured in that factory,' Percy surmised, 'and the fact that the robbery was carried out by a bunch of women. It doesn't say a great deal for your security operations, does it?'

'I'll try to convince myself that I can't detect a trace of a smirk on your aged face,' Melville said with a scowl, 'but basically you're correct. What you might wish to add to that is the fact that Home Secretary Gladstone is appalled by the possibility that women as violent and determined as that might be working for that "Votes for Women" lot. As you may be aware, things have become more and more brutal in recent confrontations between those lunatic harpies and the constables sent to prevent them causing outrages in public places, or attacking institutions such as Parliament House. It's believed that these "Suffragettes", as the press are now calling them, may have decided to seek the assistance of women who're dedicated to violence, and have been specially trained for that purpose. Your job will be to insinuate your way into those places where these women may have acquired that training, find out who they are, then line them up for hasty arrest.'

'And how might an elderly gentleman like myself acquire an introduction to a female army training establishment?' Percy asked.

Melville tutted. 'You're a master of disguise, they tell me, so just get on with it. If you need to report progress — or even lack of it — you have the telephone number for here, and you simply ask to speak to "M". Don't delay, and don't fail me.'

'And my fee?'

'Name it when you succeed — within reason, of course.'

'And if I *don't* succeed?'

'Don't even consider that possibility. Now, here comes what you inelegantly described as our "pudding". I assume you approve of plum duff with custard?'

*

There were several in Leman Street Police Station, deep in Whitechapel, who still knew Percy Enright, at least by reputation, and it had required only a simple ruse to acquire the information he needed. Posing as someone seeking to establish a 'Whitechapel Police Veterans' Association', to be presided over by himself as a former detective inspector who'd seen service there, Percy easily acquired the names of those officers who'd been rented out to the Brunner Mond factory on the night of the robbery. He also, by the same process, gained access to their photographs, and several nights later he entered the public bar of the Black Lion, tucked away halfway along Hanbury Street. He perched himself on a bar stool next to a heavily built man who looked as if the future of the world had just been placed on his broad shoulders.

'Fancy another pint?' Percy asked as he ordered one for himself.

'An' why would I wanna drink wiv you?' the man asked.

'You *are* Ted Ramsey, I assume?' Percy asked nonchalantly. 'I was given your name by Sergeant Bullimore, and I'm interested in learning as much as I can about life up the sharp end these days. I used to be on the force working out of Leman Street in the old days, and we reckoned it was rough then, but by all accounts it's got a whole lot worse. I'm writing a book that will let everyone know how tough life is for your average bobby, so that they know how valuable they are in modern society, and how they ought to be paid a lot more than they are.'

'No amount of money would make it worth what *we* goes through,' Ramsey replied sourly. 'I'll take the drink yer kindly offered, but you oughta know that I'm thinkin' o' jackin' it all in as soon as I can get a job down on the docks. The wife's insistin', yer see.'

'Surely your wife should be proud to be married to such a stout guardian of the public peace?' Percy prompted, to a responding snort of derision.

'She were 'til I come 'ome wiv me face all smashed. Look, yer can still see where they patched me up down the 'ospital, an' it ain't pretty. Then when I told 'er 'ow it 'appened, well, that were it, weren't it?'

'So how *did* it happen?'

'I were down this place along the river there — Silvertown, it's called — an' we was earning a few bob extra, private like, me an' another two o' me mates from Leman Street. We was guardin' this 'ere factory, mindin' our own business outside the front gate, when this bunch o' women come strollin' past. We thought as 'ow they was totties on their way 'ome, an' we starts ter give 'em a bit o' chinwag, like yer do, when they pulls up their skirts an' come out wiv these bloody great cudgels what was no match fer the little billy clubs we got. I went down like a sack o' spuds, an' next thing I knows I were on the back of a wagon bein' taken to the 'ospital. That one in Whitechapel Road.'

'Women, you say?' Percy asked innocently. 'That's a bit unusual, even these days, isn't it?'

'Maybe, an' maybe not,' Ramsey muttered. 'That lot what wants ter be elected fer Parliament can cut up a bit rough, an' then there are always Ma Parker an' 'er lot.'

'Ma Parker?'

'Yeah, 'er. Yer never 'eard of Ma Parker, an' you a bloke what worked on Leman Street? Musta bin after yer time there.'

'Probably. I was sent back up to the Yard after they caught the Ripper, although they never admitted that they had, because of who it was.'

'Yeah, some fancy toff, they reckons. Anyroad, Ma Parker's bin operatin' 'er little parlour fer some years, an' she's been done that often that we've given up. Every time the beaks close 'er down, she's back at it again someplace else. The latest is down Chandlers Court, off Warden Street.'

'You talking about a knocking shop?' Percy asked. 'If so, where does the violence come into it? Do the men pay to get smacked around by the totties, or what?'

'No, they pays ter watch women beltin' each other,' Ramsey replied. 'There's big money in that there prize fightin', 'specially 'cos it's not legal. An' even more so when it's women what's goin' at it.'

'No wonder you were taken by surprise,' Percy commiserated. 'Another pint?'

As the second one disappeared at the same speed as the first, Percy decided to expand his knowledge of the tactics of the Suffragettes.

'Have you actually been involved in any of those set-tos with the wild women who want the right to vote?'

'Them lot?' Ramsey replied indignantly. 'Bloody right I 'ave, up at Westminster, when we was rostered in special ter meet one o' their marches. They fights dirty, women or not, an' I don't take kindly ter bein' kicked in the plums, neither, so I belted one across the 'ead wiv me billy club. Then she 'ad the cheek ter complain as 'ow I'd "brutalised" 'er, as she called it.'

'I hope that your inspector treated that complaint with the contempt that it deserved, in the circumstances,' Percy commented in the hope of a reply, and he was not disappointed.

'The inspector never got ter 'ear about it,' Ramsey told him, ''cos it were made ter one've them women what looks after women what gets themselves arrested. "Matrons", they calls

’em. So anyroad, this woman what I’d smacked wiv me billy club complained ter this ’ere matron, an’ when I told ’er as ’ow I’d been kicked in the nuts, the matron told the woman that she only ’ad ’erself ter blame, and that were the end of it.’

‘Just to make sure that I’ve got that right,’ Percy said, ‘they’ve got women employed at police stations to look after the welfare of these Suffragette types who get themselves arrested. Is that what you’re telling me?’

‘Yeah, that’s right — matrons. Most of ’em’s the wives of bobbies, so I were ’opin’ that my Clara might put ’er ’and up fer it, but she told me she weren’t interested.’

‘Well, I’m *very* interested in what you’ve told me, Ted,’ Percy replied, ‘and I’ll make sure that it gets into my book, although I won’t mention you by name.’

‘Thank Christ fer that,’ Ramsey said, ‘since I’m in enough trouble at ’ome as it is. An’ thanks fer the drinks.’

‘You’re most welcome.’ Percy lifted himself from the bar stool and made his way outside, more than content with the results of his evening’s work for the price of two pints of indifferent beer. Now it was time to go home for some whisky and soda to take away the taste.

## CHAPTER THREE

'Do you still have a taste for chicken chow mein?' Percy asked Jack over the telephone.

Jack smiled as pleasant memories kicked in. 'I do. Did you have in mind Tang Li's, and if so, when?'

'How are you fixed today?'

'Boring recruitment interviews, but if I cut them short by revealing to the aspiring applicants what they're really letting themselves in for, I should be finished by one o'clock. Can your stomach wait that long?'

'It can for a good reason, and I believe I have one. I'll get there early and try to acquire our favourite table. My treat, which should alert you to the fact that I want something.'

'Yes — meat pie,' Jack said with a grin. 'See you at one.'

At shortly before the appointed time, Jack strolled eagerly through the front door to Tang Li's Chophouse on the Thames Embankment, to be met by a waiter with a deep bow, an ingratiating smile and a long memory for good paying customers. It had been Jack and his Uncle Percy's lunch venue of choice for some years, until Percy's choice to retire from even private investigations had no longer rendered it necessary for them to meet at lunchtimes in order that Percy might seek favours from Jack.

Quite apart from all the joint investigations that uncle and nephew had conducted over the years, officially or otherwise, Jack would always remain grateful to Percy for offering him a new start in life after his father had died, when Jack was only fourteen. He'd gone to live with Percy and Aunt Beattie in their Hackney home. It had been Percy, then a police sergeant with many a tale to tell, who'd inspired Jack to embark on a career in the Metropolitan Police, much to the displeasure of his mother Constance, who would have much preferred that Jack continued with the successful insurance brokerage business established by his father that had secured the modest family fortune.

That was now some thirty years in the past, and although in recent years they'd maintained contact by way of family Sunday lunches at the Watford house, Jack still experienced a mild shock as he looked across to where Percy had succeeded in commandeering their favourite corner table, and was now studying the menu with the selective eye of a dedicated trencherman. His face clearly showed the years that had passed, although the clear blue eyes that both the Enright brothers had inherited, and which Jack's father had passed onto him, had not dimmed. They opened wide in greeting as he saw Jack approaching the table.

'We're both in luck,' Percy said. 'They still do meat pie! Do take a seat, Jack my boy, and let's lose no time in giving the waiter something to do with his notepad.'

After they'd ordered their meals, Jack asked, 'So what are you after?'

Percy leaned forward. 'What do you know about the arrangements for ensuring the safety and security of those women who're taken into custody after attacking your colleagues on the streets?'

Jack frowned. 'You mean that "Votes for Women" lot? Have you been speaking with Esther?'

'Not lately, why?'

'Well, it's just that the mother of one of her girls at the school ended up in hospital after she confronted a bobby at some protest meeting or other. Esther's of the opinion that these women should be afforded gentle treatment, but I take the view that when they choose to take on uniformed police officers with weapons, then those officers are entitled to fight back. It's almost inevitable who's likely to come off best in a contest like that.'

Percy chuckled. 'Our paths have crossed yet again, Jack. It just so happens that our old friend William Melville has requested that I investigate the extent to which these determined ladies armed with clubs have acquired an army of trained bodyguards. I'm not allowed to reveal the precise context in which this request arises, but I've learned that there are provisions in place to ensure that those women who're arrested following these unseemly confrontations are not mishandled, sexually or otherwise.'

'I'd be surprised to learn that,' Jack replied with a shake of his head, 'given what happened to that mother at Esther's school. Although from what I can gather her injuries were sustained *on* the battlefield, as it were, and not afterwards. But what do you want me to find out for you, precisely?'

'The extent to which women are employed in local nicks in order to protect female prisoners from various forms of abuse. I'm told that they're referred to as "matrons", if that helps.'

'It doesn't, as it happens,' Jack said, frowning, 'and if there's an area of police recruitment that I'm not aware of, then I'm very concerned to hear about it. Leave it with me.'

'Your allotted duties involve recruitment of suitable young men as constables,' Chief Superintendent Barrymore reminded Jack later that day, when he asked about the ladies of whose existence Percy had made him aware over lunch. 'Why are you suddenly enquiring about matrons?'

Jack's instinct warned him not to push too hard. There had been occasions in the past when Barrymore, his ultimate superior, had queried what he regarded as Jack's unjustified enquiries into matters that were not directly connected with the duties that came with being the head of Recruitment and Manpower. A white lie seemed appropriate in the circumstances.

'It's just that one of the young men I was interviewing this morning told me that his interest in a police career had been sparked by what he'd learned from a neighbour living in the same tenement block as him, who was engaged as one of these "matrons". I had to pretend that I knew all about them, when in truth that information came as a complete revelation to me. I don't want to be caught out like that again. It doesn't look good for the head of Recruitment and Manpower not to know the full extent of our recruitment activities.'

'You're Recruitment and *Man*power, Enright, not Womanpower, but I see no reason why you shouldn't know what's common knowledge in the Yard anyway. Take a seat.'

Jack did as requested, and Barrymore spread his hands before him.

'Due to the number of women and young people who, of late, have found themselves on the wrong side of the law, it was deemed appropriate for the Met to engage suitable individuals to ensure their welfare whilst in police custody. Due to their inherent physical inferiority compared with police constables, and to avoid any unjustified allegation that this weakness has in some way been taken advantage of, it was decided that certain key police stations should have available the services of suitable ladies to ensure that there are no improprieties while women and young people are confined in the cells. At present, those allocations have been confined to those areas of the Met where there have been recent unfortunate disturbances fomented by women seeking to have the law changed to their advantage, led by those with a darker agenda. In the main, the West End and Westminster.'

'You're referring to that "Votes for Women" lot?' Jack asked.

Barrymore nodded. 'Correct, except they now seem to be referred to as "Suffragettes" by the popular newspapers, and the "Women's Social and Political Union" by their own leaders, who are believed to have a Reformist agenda that extends far beyond female suffrage.'

'And how are these matrons recruited?' Jack asked.

'It's largely ad hoc, so far as I can tell. There's certainly no recruitment programme as such, like the one you're in charge of. If there's a need for a matron to be appointed, then the senior officer in charge of the station enquires locally for anyone who may be interested. I'm led to believe, from conversations I've had with divisional superintendents, that in many cases the volunteers are wives of serving officers attached to the station in question.'

'So that they're uniquely placed to suppress any allegations against their own menfolk, or their colleagues, or to simply ignore a legitimate complaint,' Jack observed.

Barrymore's face darkened. 'Are you suggesting that the system is rigged, to employ a vulgar term?'

'Not necessarily, sir. I'm just pointing out a potential flaw in it that might be cited by anyone seeking to denigrate what in essence is an excellent arrangement — the more sensationalist of the newspapers, for example, or those who sympathise with the Suffragettes.'

'Do you have any specific examples of the system being abused?' Barrymore challenged him.

Jack recalled what Percy had told him over the top of his meat pie. 'I recently heard of a case in which a woman protestor who'd been hit over the head by a constable with a billy club was told, by one of these matrons, that her complaint was not being taken any further because she'd allegedly kicked the officer in the — well, in the private parts.'

'And if that was indeed the case, what's your concern? The matron in question demonstrated excellent judgment, and avoided wasting time on an unjustified allegation.'

'But without first enquiring into the truth of the matter, sir,' Jack pointed out. 'All that was required, in order to have the entire allegation quashed, was an assertion on the part of the constable that he'd been kicked. You can see how any prospect of officers being held to account for their misbehaviour, or even criminal actions, can be nipped in the bud with a simple lie.'

'And do you see any possible improvement for the system?' Barrymore asked tetchily. 'Is this you attempting to widen the terms of your engagement?'

'No, sir — far from it,' Jack asserted. 'I can barely keep up with the existing workload at present, given the need to ensure that the numbers joining the Met exceed those leaving it. It's just that I'm concerned that those women whose complaints are ignored without justification might seek some alternative.'

'Such as?'

'I don't know, sir. Perhaps a complaint to the newspapers, or a formal action brought by some fancy lawyer employed by the women's movement. Or even the possibility of women carrying knives into melees, for their own protection.'

'Well, we just have to hope that this doesn't happen, don't we?' Barrymore replied in a tone that hinted that the interview was over.

Jack judged that he'd pushed as far as it was safe to push. Thanking Barrymore for his time, Jack left his office and made his way back downstairs, his mind full of possibilities.

A woman with a tattooed left arm smashed her heavy fist into her opponent's face, and the woman on the receiving end flew backwards towards the temporary ring of spectators, blood from her broken nose spraying out over the nearest of them, who howled their appreciation. She was pushed back into the action by the men whose bodies effectively constituted the containment line, and she lashed out with her boot, catching her assailant in the midriff. As she doubled over, a right hook knocked her down to the already bloodstained sawdust, and it was followed by a series of kicks to her head.

Percy looked away, sickened, and asked himself for the tenth time why men would pay two pounds a head to watch this gut-churning display of brutality. He was a silent spectator inside Ma Parker's latest prize-fighting venue in courtyard tucked away off a grubby street in Whitechapel. His informant had not exaggerated about the enthusiasm with which men obviously watched this sort of thing; they were prepared to pay almost three weeks' wages for the privilege. Ma Parker herself had collected his money, commenting on the fact that this was his first time. 'If there's owt else I can supply yer wiv, darlin', just let me know,' she added. 'The girls is always willin' fer a bit of extra cash, if they ain't unconscious.'

The woman who'd been knocked to the ground appeared not to have moved since then. Ma Parker waded into the bloody circle with a stained piece of once-white cloth raised high in the air as she announced the winner to be the one still standing, albeit with blood still pouring down her upper lip and into her mouth. There was a loud cheer from the all-male audience, and obvious signs of money changing hands. Two hefty men who appeared to be part of what passed for the management of the event lifted the prone fighter from the sawdust and rolled her against the courtyard wall, where an elderly woman removed a pipe from her mouth for long enough to revive the loser by means of a bucket of filthy water thrown in her face.

The declared winner was slipped a handful of notes by Ma Parker, which she tucked down the bodice of her tattered gown with a smile. She then walked across to where a crude counter had been set up, and handed over a handful of coins in exchange for a large mug of what was probably gin. Percy had seen enough, and as two more large women stepped into the informal circle and prepared to do battle, he walked over to where the victor sat on the ground gulping down her reward, and squatted down next to her, doing his best not to inhale the stale sweat fumes.

'You fought well,' he complimented her.

She looked up at him through an eye that was half closed by the battering it had recently received, wiped blood from her upper lip, and said, 'I won't be doin' no extra business ternight, so clear off.'

'Indeed, I'm not surprised to learn that,' Percy persevered in his best upper-class accent. 'My enquiry is about whether or not you might be prepared to pass on your undoubted martial skills to my niece.'

The woman eyed him suspiciously. 'Why would a fine gentleman like you want the likes of me ter teach yer fancy niece 'ow ter kick down another woman?'

'It's a sad story,' Percy told her, having obviously engaged her interest, 'and it pains me to have to relate it, but the person against whom she would be exercising whatever martial skills you could teach her would be her husband.'

'That right?' the woman asked. 'Knocks 'er about a bit, does 'e?'

'Regrettably, yes,' Percy replied. 'And given his position in local society, no-one's inclined to believe my niece when she tries to complain to the police, or anyone else. I accepted responsibility for her when both her parents were tragically killed in a boating accident on the river, and she looks to me for her protection. I'm too old to offer her any physical safeguarding against her husband's actions, and when I saw you fighting it occurred to me that you might be able to teach her a trick or two that would cause him to desist.'

'It'll cost yer,' the woman warned him. 'Maybe five quid fer each lesson, an' it'll take a few, if she's a proper lady.'

'She is, believe me,' Percy assured her. 'So where shall I send her, or will you go to her? And what name should she ask for?'

'Me name's Ada — Ada Penny. Not me real name, but yer can't be too careful, an' yer could be a rozzer.'

'Do I *look* like a rozzer?'

'No, mainly 'cos yer too old. An' too 'oity-toity.'

'Well, there you go then. If I give you a fiver now, will you tell me where to send her?'

'I ain't gonna fall fer that,' she said. 'I tells yer where, an' the next fing I knows me place's full of rozzers. Yer can meet me, along wiv yer precious niece, at around six in the evenin' next Tuesday, outside the Bell in Brick Lane. Then she can join a class what I'll be 'oldin' fer a few other ladies o' quality what needs ter defend 'emselves against their menfolk, or them bobbies what likes ter chance their arm when there's nobody lookin'.'

'The ones who're trying to persuade Parliament to give them the vote?'

'None o' yourn, so let's just say next Tuesday, six o'clock, the Bell. An' I'll take that there fiver on account.'

Percy handed over a five pound note from his wallet, and Ada grabbed it easily, then grinned as she began to pick the dried blood from her upper lip.

'It's got ter be better than this line o' work, anyroad. See yer Tuesday, an' bring another fiver wiv yer. That one were just fer the introduction, in a manner o' speakin'.'

The following morning Jack was barely behind his desk at work when the phone rang, and he was offered an incoming call. Since his was an internal line that was connected by way of the main switchboard, he could refuse to take it, but he'd never yet denied the uncle to whom he owed everything.

'Good morning, Uncle Percy. Booking another lunch meeting, are we?'

'We are, but not at Tang Li's, and not today,' Percy replied. 'Does your memory go back far enough to those family Sunday lunches you used to host? And does your generosity extend to hosting another one this coming Sunday? If so, please invite Lucy and Teddy as well, because I have a feeling that not even Esther will agree to what I need.'

# CHAPTER FOUR

'I still say they've only got themselves to blame,' Jack insisted.

Esther responded with a snort of disapproval. 'Spoken like a hardened police officer! These are *women* we're talking about — wives, mothers, sisters — not to mention children. "The weaker sex", they call us, when they're seeking to minimise our importance in society. But when it comes to some of our gender seeking to argue for a greater role in that society, suddenly they're so dangerous to the public peace that they have to be battered with billy clubs, dragged along the muddy ground by their hair, and sexually abused when they're taken down into the privacy of a grubby police cell.'

'We don't know that they're sexually abused,' Jack countered. 'And before you tell me that you read it in *The Pall Mall Gazette*, or another of those mouthpieces for trouble-stirrers, let me remind you that you were the one who warned me against believing everything that you read in the newspapers.'

It was Sunday lunchtime around the family table in the dining room of 'The Lodge' in Watford, and everyone was there except Beattie. She had accompanied Annabelle and Lily as a chaperone while they took a picnic and went to watch Bertie's battalion marching to Bushey Heath, where they were to proudly display their skills in mock combat. The meal was only halfway consumed, because as everyone began to express an opinion on the issue of female suffrage it had somehow degenerated into a heated exchange regarding the current tactics being employed by the Suffragettes. Even Percy had left his roast pork half-eaten on the plate in front of him.

The rot had begun to set in when Percy had asked Jack what he'd learned about the function of the matrons employed inside selected police stations. Jack had pointed out the potential flaw in the system resulting from recruitment into the matrons being largely restricted to those more likely to be sympathetic to the actions of the police.

Esther had reacted angrily: 'Think of poor little Clarissa Melrose, whose mother may never be released from hospital because of what some police brute was allowed to inflict on her with his billy club!' It was in response to this that Jack had expressed the opinion that women who chose to take on police officers in a physical way only had themselves to blame.

Percy chortled as he threw in his tuppenceworth. 'The women I saw punching and kicking the stuffing out of each other a few evenings ago had nothing to fear from police officers, from what I could judge. I'm only too glad that devils like those didn't haunt the streets in my younger uniformed days.'

'Doesn't that disqualify them as women, though?' Teddy Masefield asked, and his wife, Lucy — Jack's younger sister — was the next to snort derisively.

'They don't cease to be women, just because they stand up for themselves, Teddy. Power to them, I say! Perhaps once they manage to get round the obvious problem arising from women being physically weaker than men, they'll get more respect from the so-called "stronger sex". At present, so far as I can tell, the only thing that prevents these Suffragette types from being heard, and conveying a *very* important message to the world regarding the need for equality between the sexes in matters of public life, is the ability of bully boy police officers to shut them up using mindless violence.'

'Hear! Hear!' Esther muttered. 'Now please finish off your main courses, all of you, if you want some of that delicious apple pie that's probably going cold on the kitchen table.'

They resumed eating, and nothing more was said on the subject of the campaign for women's equality until they were back in the sitting room, drinking tea, and Jack asked quietly of Percy, 'How brutal *were* those women you referred to earlier?'

'I was pretty well sickened by what I saw,' Percy admitted, 'but the interesting thing that I learned from it is that one of them, using the false name of "Ada Penny", is offering self-defence classes for women whose husbands knock them around at home. More to the point, she hinted that she was giving the same instruction to the more militant Suffragettes who find themselves taking on police officers.'

'Good!' Lucy smiled as she stirred the sugar into her tea. 'Particularly the bit about married women being trained to resist physical abuse from their husbands. One hears *far* too much about that sort of things these days, and from what I've gathered the police just refuse to take their complaints seriously.'

'I trust that you're not speaking from personal experience?' Jack asked.

Lucy shook her head. 'Of course not — Teddy's a perfect gentleman. But I'd have wanted to defend myself if he'd turned into one of those domestic brutes that I sometimes hear about among my theatrical friends. They're all sweetness and kind consideration during their courting days, and in the early months of marriage, but then the first time they have a serious disagreement, out come the fists. If you ask me, one of the root causes of women seeking a greater say in society is in order to require the authorities to take matters more seriously when a long-suffering wife finally plucks up the courage to complain about her husband's physical abuse of her.'

It fell awkwardly silent, until Esther said, in a small voice, 'I think there's more to it than that, Lucy. I obviously hear what you say about physical violence within a marriage, but these Suffragettes are demanding much more than protection from that. In fact, what they're asking for could be interpreted as a challenge to men's established positions of authority, and you can perhaps see — while not necessarily agreeing with it — why men are reacting in the way that they are.'

'Whose side are you on?' Lucy challenged her. 'Do you actually *want* women to remain the downtrodden half of society? It's all very well for you, because you've attained a position of respect and authority since you were fortunate enough to meet a very strong woman who dragged you along behind her.'

'Also because I'm good at what I do,' Esther replied, bristling, and Percy chose this moment to leap to his niece's defence.

'Lucy's not denying that, Esther. The point she's making is that when circumstances opened up for you to take advantage of your natural abilities, you had a mentor who herself was a perfect role model for other women, and a husband who was quite happy to see you develop as an individual, as well as fulfilling your role as a wife and mother. Lucy's point is that there are many others who will never be as fortunate as you, and she'd like to see their cause advanced.'

'Precisely, Uncle Percy,' Lucy said gratefully, 'and I'm really sorry if I gave the wrong impression, Esther. I wasn't denigrating your talents or hard work, honestly I wasn't. It's just that apart from my entirely voluntary and amateur work in the local theatre, I've never had the chance to shine like you have, given the limitations placed on career opportunities for women — even ones with the benefit of a good education.'

'And you would of course take any opportunity that presents itself to assist in removing those limitations?' Percy asked slyly.

Lucy nodded. 'Of course,' she agreed.

Esther gave Percy a suspicious stare before advising her, 'Have a care, Lucy. Uncle Percy's using his "follow me over this trapdoor" voice, and experience tells me that he's about to back you into a corner from which you can only escape by volunteering for one of his underhanded stunts.'

'I wouldn't dream of asking Lucy to partake in something that's probably beyond her capability or courage,' Percy insisted with a wry smile in Jack's direction.

'You haven't told me what it might be yet,' Lucy objected. 'I'll be the judge of what's beyond me and what isn't, so what did you have in mind?'

'Hook, line and sinker,' Esther muttered, as Percy began to explain.

'Well, I hadn't mentioned it up until now, but I was looking for some way to infiltrate this group of women who're receiving training in how to defend themselves. I'm sure that most of them are housewives who aren't as fortunate as you to have such a splendid husband as Teddy, but some of them may also be hoping to use that training against bobbies during street protests. All I'd need would be for you to pose as a mistreated housewife, so you can strike up conversations with the other women there and try to find out if their intended targets are likely to be wearing police uniforms.'

'Shouldn't you ask Teddy if he minds you taking such an awful risk?' Esther asked, to a chuckle from Teddy himself.

'If she needed my permission to do that, then she probably *would* need to seek support in order to assert her independence,' he reminded Esther, who nodded, blushed, then fell silent.

'Where and when?' Lucy asked of Percy.

'This coming Tuesday, six o'clock in the evening, outside the Bell Inn in Brick Lane, which is on the boundary of Spitalfields and Whitechapel.'

'And *very* rough,' Esther told her. 'If you see a cat there with a tail, it's wandered in from another district. Believe me, I know — I used to live in that area.'

'Before your fortunes improved out of sight,' Lucy replied. 'I'll be doing this for those who didn't have your advantages or good fortune.'

'I'm delighted to hear that you've agreed to help,' Percy encouraged, 'but you won't be going down there alone. Be at our house by five o'clock, and we'll take the omnibus down to Shoreditch from there.'

'And good luck,' Esther added, then looked up expectantly as the sitting room door opened and Bertie appeared. His hair was plastered to his head, there were grass stains and mud on his khaki tunic, and his belt webbing was cut.

'We beat the First Battalion into a cocked hat!' he announced proudly. 'The earl says we're a credit to the regiment!'

'He doesn't have to repair your uniform,' Esther said sourly. 'And what have you done with your admirers?'

'Right behind him,' Annabelle announced, as her smiling face appeared from behind Bertie. 'Lily's washing her hands, because she fell down in some mud, and Polly's dabbing it off her dress.'

'Fortunately their Aunt Beatrice came to no harm,' Beattie assured them as she walked into the sitting room, her parasol over her arm. 'The rain held off, and the picnic that Polly provided proved to be excellent. But I'd be very grateful for a cup of tea.'

Esther lost no time in supplying it, then offered her one of the jam tarts that remained on the plate as an after-lunch treat.

'No thank you,' she said. 'However, there is one favour you might consider, if it's in order with you. While we were having our picnic, Annabelle and Lily were asking all about life in London, and it suddenly occurred to me that since you moved up here to Watford all those years ago, only Annabelle's had any exposure to London life, and even then only during occasional holidays with us. I was wondering if you might be prepared to allow the two of them to stay with Percy and myself for a few days, during which I can show them the sights, and perhaps take them window shopping in Regent Street and Bond Street.'

'I can't see any harm in that,' Esther replied, 'and I won't even give Jack the opportunity to object, since he's become quite a stick in the mud of late.'

'With just cause,' Jack muttered, 'given my hopeless workload, and the task of topping up police recruit numbers as more and more of them resign, or get injured by those women who my little sister will be meeting with. Anyway, I think Percy must be ready for a pipe, so we'll take a turn together in the garden.'

Percy was puffing contentedly on his pipe and admiring the hedge that separated Jack's garden from Cassiobury Park when Jack gave a chuckle.

'You haven't got any less tricky with age,' he observed. 'Lucy fell for that one like a ton of bricks.'

'She's not as experienced as Esther in spotting a trap,' Percy told him, then the smile suddenly faded. 'I just hope I haven't overstretched myself this time, and led her into real danger.'

*

'Yer remembered, then,' Ada Penny observed as she left the Bell Inn, wiping foam from her lips. She looked intently at Lucy. 'Yer looks fit enough fer me ter teach yer what yer needs ter know, but remember that it ain't ter do wiv 'ow tough yer are — it's 'ow yer does it, an' where it 'urts most. Yer doesn't mind givin' yer old man a lotta pain, I take it?'

'It'll be no more than he's given me over the past few years, the bastard,' Lucy replied bitterly, surprising even Percy, who stood silently by her side.

'Yer can come wiv us ter the door, then yer'll need ter sling yer 'ook,' Ada told Percy. 'An' if yer comes back wiv rozzers, God 'elp yer, 'cos yer'll be takin' on a room full o' women what knows the score. Right, off we goes.'

She led them through several mean side streets until they came to an abandoned shop premises halfway down White's Row. The single window was boarded over with a sheet of thin wood that was permanently stained from months' worth of rain, and the door was opened from the inside when Ada knocked five times on it.

'They used ter sell 'orsemeat in 'ere,' she told Lucy as Percy hung back on the pavement, 'then the bloke what owned it drank himself ter death, an' 'is widder rents it out fer lots of different uses. I got it fer Tuesday nights, an' as yer can see, yer not the only one who comes.'

Lucy stepped inside the relatively large room that was lit only by the faint light from a moderate fire burning in a grate, around which half a dozen women were huddling. At first glance, they looked to be respectable, middle-aged and rather shamefaced, and Ada's first action was to collect five pounds from each of them, Lucy included. Then she smiled and began the evening's class.

'First of all, say 'ello to another lady what wants ter learn 'er 'usband some respect the next time 'e fancies givin' 'er a smack. 'Er name's Lucy, so make 'er welcome.'

The other ladies gave Lucy either a nod or a somewhat embarrassed smile.

'Stand in yer usual line,' Ada instructed them. 'Lucy, you just stand on the end of it, while we goes back over what they learned last week.'

Lucy did as instructed, then listened attentively as Ada reminded them of how to break the arm of someone coming towards a victim with a knife or a club. Lucy was obliged to hide her wince of horror as she learned how easy it was, simply by forcing the arm back on itself at the elbow, then snapping it over a raised knee, as if breaking a branch to make kindling for a fire. Then it was on to simple footwork, stepping to one side as an opponent approached, sticking a leg out in front of them, then pushing the victim head-first over the obstacle by reaching behind them. Finally, Ada mimed a series of well delivered finger stabs to various places on the neck and face, including an eyeball, all designed to incapacitate an opponent for long enough to make a hasty escape.

'Let's just take a rest fer a minute, shall we?' Ada suggested, and several of those in attendance lowered themselves onto the floorboards after first dusting them with a rag that was kept in a corner for that very purpose. Ada herself extracted a hip flask from the bag that she'd been carrying ever since leaving the Bell, and drank from it eagerly. One lady handed round a bag of cashews, while two others who appeared to be sisters shared a tin of cough lozenges.

A well-padded, but well preserved, lady who'd been making Lucy feel uncomfortable by watching her closely during the instruction they'd just received sat down next to her. 'Are you really here because your husband beats you, or do you have some other reason for learning how to defend yourself?' she asked.

'What other reason might I have?' Lucy hedged. 'And may I take it that you *do*?'

'It's just that you don't look like the downtrodden sort. Pardon my presumption — my name's Charlotte, by the way. "Charlie" to my husband, and "Lottie" among certain friends who want me to be able to come to their defence when needed. I thought you might have been sent by Christabel.'

'I don't think I know anyone by that name,' Lucy replied, 'and I'm here because I'm tired of being used as a doormat.'

'Yes, I know the feeling,' Charlotte commiserated. 'I went through the same for a year or two, then threatened to leave the brute if he hit me one more time. I also told my brother what was going on, and he threatened to horsewhip him if it happened again. It was a pity that I needed a man to stand up for me, but it was my only option at the time. However, those times are rapidly coming to an end, and my friends — the ones I'm here to learn to defend — have set certain processes in train that will give us women much greater control over how we're regarded and treated by men. Might you be interested in learning more?'

'I might,' Lucy said with a smile, 'but not until I've had a chance to try what I've learned this evening on my rat of a husband. If I come back here next Tuesday, will you be here again?'

'Depend upon it,' Charlotte assured her, 'then I'll introduce you to some of my friends here. There are two others among us this evening.'

Ada called them all back at this point, and the lesson continued for another half hour or so, during which Lucy learned how to scrape the heel of her boot down the front of a man's shinbone, in what they were assured was a most painful means of putting even a big strong man off his stride. Then with thanks for an enlightening evening, and a few nodded farewells, they all made their way back outside. Charlotte was alongside Lucy as they stepped out into the darkness of White's Row, and she stopped dead when she saw Percy lurking in the shadows.

'Don't be afraid,' Lucy reassured her. 'This man's my Uncle Percy, and he's paying for my lessons. He hates my husband for what he does to me, and he's looked after my interests ever since my parents died. He's obviously too old to give Teddy — that's my husband — the thrashing he deserves, but this is his way of helping me.'

'So this kindly old man's interested in supporting women against the brutality and arrogance of men, is he?' Charlotte asked. 'If so, we might find a use for him.'

'We?' Percy echoed as he caught what she was saying.

Charlotte smiled, leaned forward and gave Percy a kiss on the cheek. 'My friends,' she replied. 'Lucy will explain, and hopefully I'll see you *both* next week. Now, I've just got time to hail a cab in Commercial Street, so I'll bid you both a good evening.'

As she walked briskly away, Lucy took Percy's arm.

'It sounds as if you had a fruitful time in there, so let's head in the opposite direction,' he said. 'There's a cab stand in Bell Lane. From the look of triumph on your face, I'll take a guess that you have a lot to tell this "kindly old man" that needs to be kept private, and you've certainly earned a better journey home than a ride in an omnibus.'

# CHAPTER FIVE

Lily and Annabelle stood, transfixed and wide-eyed, on the pavement halfway down Oxford Street, as they gazed up at the tall columns of the building in front of them that reminded them of photographs they'd seen of Greek monuments. They then let their attention drift down through the wide glass window panels to the bustling scene inside, where there were more people, mainly women, in one place than either of them had ever seen. Beattie smiled at their wonderment, although even she was impressed. It was the first time she'd laid eyes on this latest shopping palace, because it had been open for barely four months.

'Are we allowed to go inside?' Lily asked, to a smile and a nod from Beattie.

'Of course — that's what Mr Selfridge wants us to do, and by all accounts there's no obligation to purchase anything.'

It was totally unlike any shop that either girl had experienced before, and even for Beattie it was an eye-opener, and the last word in luxury. A small string quartet played softly in one corner of the ground floor, while a fountain of coloured water cascaded gently into a rock pool in another. The glass-topped counters close to the entrance displayed luxury items such as perfumes, soaps, costume jewellery and ladies' watches. Wherever they looked, signs directed them to upper floors where they could admire clothing, haberdashery and lace goods, accessed by means of metal tubes called elevators that were operated by smartly uniformed attendants, and took the customers from one level to another inside a closed compartment that Lily and Annabelle were too nervous to experience, so they used the ornate staircases instead.

Behind each shiny counter was a small group of young female sales assistants, clad in crisp white blouses and long black skirts, and ready to answer any question they might have regarding the merchandise on display with a ready smile. They spent almost an hour admiring the goods on sale, but dared not ask how much they cost, since none of the items seemed to bear a price tag. Eventually they walked back out with reluctance, but Beattie told them that there was much more of London for them to see.

By the time they'd wandered, equally entranced, down past all the smaller stores in Bond Street, admiring the window displays of jewellery in particular, Beattie suggested that they make their way further down, to Piccadilly Circus. There they rested their weary feet on the steps at the foot of what was officially known as the Shaftesbury Memorial Fountain, but more popularly referred to as the Eros statue. They watched the bustling traffic negotiating the centre island, most of it horsedrawn, but a few of the new internal combustion engines powered omnibuses and wagons, belching out fumes that caught in their throats.

Beattie took out her watch, studied it briefly, then asked, 'Are you two girls hungry?' They eagerly confirmed that they were, so she led them down through Haymarket, with its famous theatres lining both sides of the street, until they reached a moderate-sized café called the Georgian Tea House.

'Your Uncle Percy used to bring me here during our courting days,' she told them as they sat down at a table near the back and studied the neatly written menu cards. 'We can rest before we venture any further. Feel free to order whatever takes your fancy.'

While they indulged themselves with éclairs, fruit tarts and puff pastry, washed down with Darjeeling tea that was a first for both girls, they gazed in fascination at the exotic characters who made up the majority of the café's clientele. Most were theatre types in wide-brimmed hats, baggy trousers known as plus fours, and gaily coloured loose jackets. Then Beattie asked if her charges had enough energy left to walk a little further before catching their omnibus back to Hackney.

'Of course, Aunt Beattie,' Annabelle answered for them both. 'Where did you have in mind?'

'Well, have either of you seen Trafalgar Square, with its statue of Lord Nelson?' she asked.

'I have,' Lily replied, 'but only in a school book, and I'd *love* to actually stand under the column and look up. They say that you can feed the pigeons as well — is that true?'

'It was when I was last there,' Beattie told her. 'Then I thought we might walk down Whitehall towards the Embankment, and see where your father works, in Scotland Yard. We'll pass Downing Street on the way, which is where the Prime Minister lives.'

'This is all *so* exciting!' Annabelle declared. 'When we get home, I'm going to write all about it — a story called "An Orphan Girl Explores London". Thank you *so* much, Aunt Beattie.'

'It's a pleasure,' Beattie replied with a loving smile. 'I often dreamed about showing a daughter of my own around the city I grew up in, and although that wasn't meant to be, escorting my two grandnieces is just as rewarding. So, if you've finished eating, let's beckon the waitress over for our bill.'

They were halfway down Whitehall, with imposing buildings on both sides that sightseers were admiring, when they became aware of some sort of disturbance further down Horse Guards

Avenue, which led off Whitehall to their left. A crowd had gathered, and was half blocking the entrance to the side street, chattering excitedly and pointing to what was taking place further down, in front of another Government building. Then behind them, from the direction of Trafalgar Square, where Beattie and the girls had just spent a pleasant half hour, came three horsedrawn police wagons, followed by half a dozen mounted police officers. The procession swung quickly into Horse Guards Avenue, narrowly missing several of the gawping spectators on its corner, then continued at a smart gallop towards the Government building halfway down on the left, outside which a large group of women had gathered.

Annabelle and Lily raced ahead of Beattie, despite her stern admonition to stay back. They were in time to see that the women outside the building were angrily waving placards and yelling for urgent reform of the law. Then two of the women stepped forward from the front row and began hurling rocks at the side windows of the building, which lay only a few feet away, behind a set of railings. The crash of broken glass provoked a loud cheer from the main body of the women, as the first two then ran round to the front of the same building and launched more rocks at its front windows.

Several more rocks had found their target before the police reinforcements arrived in order to supplement the almost token police guard at the front door, and what followed would have been beyond Annabelle and Lily's belief, had they not witnessed it for themselves.

Two of the mounted police urged their horses into a gallop towards the women who'd been throwing the rocks, and knocked them flat. They skidded across the rough ground, their long skirts riding up their thighs in an immodest display of undergarments, and several uniformed constables dashed from the hastily opened rear door of the leading police transport and began attacking their heads with drawn billy clubs.

Annabelle gave a scream as she convinced herself for a moment that the two women must be dead, then gasped when she saw them both being pulled from the ground by their hair and thrown into an empty police wagon that had been drawn up to one side. Several women had attempted to rescue their companions, but had themselves been beaten to the ground by blows repeatedly inflicted by grinning bobbies wielding billy clubs. There were soon half a dozen women lying on the dirty ground, but after making no effort to arrest any of them, the police walked swiftly back to their transport wagon, sliding their clubs into the leather belt attachments in which they were normally housed. The wagon was then turned and driven back into Whitehall at high speed.

'That was *monstrous*!' Annabelle shouted as she raced forward, despite a strident call from Beattie.

'Stay well out of it!' Beattie urged. 'You'll get yourself killed!'

Annabelle took no notice and was followed by Lily, who made her way over to where one of the unconscious women was being tended to by a middle-aged lady wearing a sash on which was written 'Medical Orderly'.

'Is she dead?' Lily asked in horror.

The woman shook her head. 'Just out cold,' she assured Lily. 'Watch.'

She extracted a bottle of something from her jacket pocket, uncorked it, then held it under the woman's nose. She coughed and retched, then her eyes opened as if in surprise, and her saviour grinned as she looked back up at Lily.

'Smelling salts — never known them to fail. If she'd been dead, she wouldn't have responded to them like that.'

'But how did you know that she *wasn't* dead — before that, I mean?' Lily asked.

The woman shrugged. 'Experience. That and the fact that I could smell aniseed balls. She must have been sucking on one when she got knocked down, and I could smell it on her breath, which meant that she was breathing out, and therefore still alive.' She turned to the injured woman. 'Now then, dear, does it hurt anywhere other than your head?'

'My right arm,' the woman complained. 'It hurts like Hell, and I think it's busted.'

'Can you move your fingers?' the orderly asked, and the woman demonstrated that she could.

'It's not broken, then — just bruised or badly sprained,' she was told. 'Now, if this young lady would help me for a moment, we'll soon get you in a fit state to see a doctor when you get home.' She looked at Lily and instructed, 'Here, hold the lady's arm tightly against her side while I strap it up tight with this bandage. That'll keep it good and steady for a while, anyway.'

'Are you a doctor?' Lily asked, fascinated by the woman's confidence and calmness, while all around them were the sounds of outrage and distress.

'How can I be?' came the testy response. 'I'm not a man, am I?'

'Why do you need to be a man to be a doctor?' Lily asked. 'Surely it's a matter of how clever you are, not whether you're a man or a woman?'

'Tell that to that lot in the Government,' the woman said with a snort. 'And you've got a lot to learn about how the world works. You've got to be a man to be a doctor, or for that matter a lawyer, a dentist or a politician.'

'So if you're not a doctor, are you a nurse?'

'I was going to be, and I did my first year of training. Then they told me that I'd been "deemed unsuitable for nursing", didn't they?'

'But you did a very good job of looking after this lady,' Lily objected.

'That was just basic nursing — and some of these other ladies look as if they're going to need more than that, so excuse me while I go and see what I can do for them. Unless you want to come with me and learn how it's done?'

Without another word the woman began picking her way through the fallen, some of whom she was able to revive, some of whom remained unconscious and would require what the woman described as 'proper attention'. The woman was able to treat minor head wounds, bandaging them after cleaning dirt and other detritus from the open cuts, assisted by Lily, who handed her what she called for from out of the heavy portmanteau that went with her everywhere.

'You're quite good at this, for a young girl,' the woman commented after Lily had assisted with the third head wound. 'What's your name?'

'Lily, short for "Lillian". Lillian Enright.'

'Well, Lillian Enright, my name's Sarah. Sarah Millichip.'

'Why were you "deemed unsuitable for nursing"?' Lily asked bluntly.

Sarah gave her a wan smile. 'I was with this lot.' She indicated with a wide sweep of her hand around what looked like the aftermath of a battle. 'We were simply asking for the Government to allow women the right to vote — out on Ealing Common, it was. I was arrested and convicted of assaulting a police officer, which I didn't, but they said I did, and that was enough. I got fourteen days in a dreadful damp cell, then, when I got back to the hospital where I was training

— Chelsea, it was — I was told that I wasn't fit to be a nurse, and that my training had been cancelled. But by then I'd learned a few basic things, and so I'm able to help others, like the ones we've treated this morning. There's a few like me, and we do what we can for our "Sisters in Progress", as I like to call them. You didn't seem too disturbed by what you saw, and you didn't faint when dressing wounds or anything, so you might want to join us in helping those who need a bit of basic medical assistance when those bully boys get stuck into them.'

'There you are!' came a familiar voice from just behind them, and Lily looked up into the face of a very concerned and annoyed Aunt Beattie. 'I've been looking for you everywhere. There are so many women lying around in various states of disorder that I thought you might be one of them. And where's Annabelle got to?'

'No idea, Aunt Beattie — and sorry that I went missing. I've been helping this kind lady give assistance to those of her friends who were attacked by those awful police constables.'

'No more than they deserved,' Beattie said dismissively, 'throwing things at windows like that. And let me remind you that both your Uncle Percy *and* your father were once police constables.'

'I hope they didn't behave like the ones who knocked these ladies to the ground,' Lily replied.

Sarah sniffed as she turned to walk away. 'I didn't realise I was keeping company with the enemy. Shame, really — thanks for your help.'

'What did she mean by "the enemy"?' Beattie demanded as she watched Sarah striding away with her portmanteau. 'And what's in that bag she's carrying?'

'Things to help women who get knocked down by police constables with weapons,' Lily replied. 'And I think it was those whom she was calling "the enemy". Me included, it seems.'

'Well, this is clearly no place for us to be dawdling,' Beattie announced, 'so as soon as we find Annabelle, we'd better make our way down to the Embankment and enquire about an omnibus back to Hackney. Now, can you see her anywhere?'

Annabelle was eventually located halfway up the former York Place, which ran off Horse Guards Avenue at right angles to it. She was among a group of women who'd beaten a hasty retreat at the first sign of the police attack, and they were complaining bitterly about the treatment they'd received.

'Someone should tell the newspapers,' one woman said, and Annabelle's ears pricked up.

'Complete waste of time!' another woman retorted. 'They don't want the truth — only stuff that'll please their editors, else it won't get printed. And if those who own the papers don't like what they read, someone's out of a job. And no-one wants to read that the police are a load of bullies who attack helpless women, do they?'

'Well, they should, if it's the truth!' Annabelle blurted out without thinking, and several pairs of eyes were turned on her.

'And who are *you*?' one of them demanded. 'One of those police snoopers?'

'I didn't know they had any,' Annabelle admitted, suddenly embarrassed. 'I was just saying that the public should know all about what those awful police constables did to your friends who were dragged away by their hair. What were their names?'

'See — she's a snooper!' the same woman insisted.

'Well, she isn't likely to find out anything that won't be in tomorrow's papers, when they appear in court,' an older woman observed. 'Why do you want their names, young lady?'

'Because I intend to write a story all about what I saw today,' Annabelle announced, inspired by what she'd witnessed, but unsure of whether or not she could get her story published. 'From what I heard somebody say just now, the newspapers won't print the truth — is that right?'

'It most certainly is,' the older woman confirmed, 'but that shouldn't stop you trying. And we need all the help we can get to bring the truth to the public's attention. My name is Sylvia Pankhurst — what's yours?'

'Annabelle. Annabelle Pickering.'

'Well, good luck to you in your attempt to get the truth before the general public,' Sylvia replied. 'The two ladies who were arrested were called Ada Wright and Sarah Carwin, and they'll no doubt appear in Bow Street Magistrates Court in the morning, charged with breaking Government windows — and no doubt assaulting the police as well.'

'But surely *they* were the ones who were assaulted — and *very* brutally — by the police?' Annabelle argued.

Sylvia let out a cynical laugh. 'Welcome to the truth, dear — now go away and write about it.'

'I definitely will,' Annabelle promised, then heard a strident but familiar voice calling her name. She looked back up into Horse Guards Avenue, where a red-faced Aunt Beattie was beckoning imperiously, with an apprehensive-looking Lily standing beside her.

'I have to go now,' she told Sylvia. 'That's my aunt calling to me — I'm probably in trouble just for talking to you.'

'It could be worse,' Sylvia told her. 'It could be your uncle.'

For the entire uncomfortable journey back to Hackney, which involved two changes of omnibus, Aunt Beattie kept up a tirade against what they had done. 'You showed disgraceful disobedience, ruining what had up until then been a perfect day out. I shall be very reluctant to take you on any further expeditions into the city, and I shall not hesitate to advise your father and granduncle of your appalling behaviour. Then I'll be sending you home.'

When they reached Hackney, Beattie made a point of telephoning Jack at work, and unburdening herself of her outrage at the impetuosity of the two girls. She then insisted that Percy accompany the girls to Euston and ensure that they took the next available train back to Watford.

'What do you think Uncle Jack will say? Will he punish us?' Annabelle asked as they watched Harrow pass by through their carriage window.

'I don't know, and I don't care,' Lily replied. 'I think I want to learn how to be a nurse, anyway, whatever he says.'

'And I'm going to write to the newspapers with the truth,' Annabelle asserted, her jaw set in determination.

# CHAPTER SIX

Annabelle and Lily stood, heads bowed and duly contrite, as Jack and Esther confronted them in the sitting room as soon as they'd washed and come back downstairs ahead of supper.

'What possessed you?' Jack demanded. 'Those women are capable of attacking police officers, smashing windows and stealing explosives for use against those who stand in the way of their demands. Aunt Beattie tells me that you rushed into the thick of it, despite her instruction to stay well away. What did you think you were about?'

'We didn't mean any harm, or intend to be naughty, Papa,' Lily wheedled. 'It was just *so* fascinating, and we couldn't get a clear look at what was going on because of the large crowd that had gathered.'

'A dissident mob, you mean?' Jack raged, and this time it was Annabelle who offered what justification she could for their behaviour.

'They weren't exactly a mob, Uncle Jack. Admittedly, they were throwing stones at windows, but what the police did next was atrocious. They first of all knocked two women down with their horses, and when others tried to rescue them some other bobbies began beating the women around the head with their truncheons.'

'Billy clubs,' Jack corrected her. 'They're called "billy clubs", and from what I've been told they needed them for their own protection, because some of those women have been taught how to fight back.'

'They wouldn't *need* to fight back if they weren't being attacked viciously in the first place,' Annabelle reasoned.

Jack's face grew red. 'Are you actually justifying what those women were doing — hurling rocks through the windows of public buildings?'

'No, of course not,' Annabelle replied, 'but nor can *you* justify what the police were doing. Is that what you train them to do?'

'That's quite *enough*, Annabelle!' Esther insisted, alarmed at the argument that was only one accusation away. 'Is what Annabelle's saying true, Lily? Did the police *really* set about those women with their clubs?'

'Annabelle's not a liar,' Lily insisted. 'I saw it with my own eyes as well. They were lucky that they didn't kill anyone — as far as I know, anyway — and I watched while one lovely lady went round the ones who'd been knocked to the ground, giving them what medical assistance she could, with a little help from me.'

'You did *what*?' Jack all but shouted. 'You actually joined in on the side of that mob of rioters?'

'Annabelle's already made it clear that they weren't rioting, dear,' Esther reminded him calmly. 'But Aunt Beattie made no mention of the brutal police behaviour that both girls clearly saw for themselves, which no doubt explains why she was so outraged by the girls' actions. It really *was* remiss of you both to disobey Aunt Beattie like that, and she's insisting that there are to be no more trips into London — not accompanied by her, anyway.'

Both girls sighed with disappointment.

'It was turning out to be the best day we'd had for ages,' said Annabelle. 'It's no fun stuck up here in Watford, day after day, and I for one found what we saw in London *fascinating*. So much history, so much grandeur, and so much to occupy our attention. I'd love to see more of it, but I suppose it's back here in boring old Watford for the foreseeable future.'

'I've been meaning to raise that with you for some time now,' Esther replied, 'but given my distraction with the need to promote the school, I haven't been able to think it through. You both left school years ago, and you've been moping around the house ever since. Do you have any idea what you'd like to do with your lives?'

'I want to be a writer,' Annabelle told her. 'Perhaps writing books about the history of London.'

'And I'd like to study to become a doctor or nurse,' Lily added. 'While I was helping that woman go to the assistance of the other women who'd been knocked down, I got a strong feeling that I'd like to be doing that — you know, helping sick people.'

'Well, you can forget becoming a doctor,' Jack told her coldly, though his anger appeared to have abated. 'The profession is only open to men, or so I'm told.'

'Isn't that why these women are driven to throwing stones at windows?' Annabelle challenged him. 'Because they're barred from so many interesting professions?'

'That's as may be,' Esther intervened quickly, 'but Lily could still study to become a nurse.'

'Where could I study for that?' Lily asked hopefully.

Esther shrugged. 'I've no idea at present, but I could make enquiries.'

'And where might I do the necessary background reading to write a book about the history of London?' Annabelle asked listlessly. 'I'm sure the local library won't have the books I'd need.'

'The same for me, with medical books,' Lily said with a sigh.

Jack had been thinking, and remembering several conversations he'd had with a man who travelled regularly in the same railway carriage as him every morning. 'If you're both looking for a library, and if it will put an end to the boredom that clearly led you both astray, I may have a solution,' he said. 'There's a man who travels on the train with me almost every morning who tells me that he's a librarian. I've never really paid much attention to his chatter, but he seems most knowledgeable about so many things that we've talked about — the geography of the world, the kings of England, the oceans and so on. Perhaps he'll be able to recommend somewhere where you might both spend your time studying. I think his library isn't far from Euston, because he once told me that he only has a ten-minute walk ahead of him when we reach the terminus. Would you like me to make further enquiry of him?'

Both girls accepted Jack's offer with enthusiasm, and were eagerly awaiting his return the following evening. He told them his news almost as soon as he walked through the door.

'The man's name is Claude Davenport, and he's Assistant Chief Curator at a place called the British Museum Library, down the road from Euston Station. He's agreeable to you attending the library every day, and you can travel down with us on the train, if you're prepared to breakfast early and take the seven-twenty with me. I'll provide you with money to buy your lunches somewhere close by, and if it doesn't work out, well, there's nothing lost, is there?'

'That sounds like an admirable idea,' Esther enthused, 'and if they don't find a suitable place for their lunches, Polly can always supply them with sandwiches. That area of London's quiet and respectable enough, and they can make sure that they're there to meet you at the station for the train home. What do you say, young ladies?'

'Oh, yes please!' they replied, almost in unison, and Annabelle gave Esther a big hug.

'Thank you *so* much for being my teacher, then my sort of aunt, and — well, can I say it? — my sort of *mother*!'

'It's been a great pleasure,' Esther assured her as she swallowed a tear. 'Just take full advantage of these opportunities that are opening up for you, that's all I ask.'

'Where do we start?' Lily asked in a whisper, totally overawed by the sheer number of volumes on the shelves by which they were surrounded. They were sitting beside each other in the General Reading Room of the British Museum Library, in which they'd been allocated seats, and to which they'd been supplied with admission cards.

'I don't know about you,' Annabelle whispered back, 'but I'm going to take a look through that stack of newspapers on that stand over there, and see how they reported on that appalling spectacle we witnessed in Whitehall.'

By the time Lily had found a book that promised to give her some basic information about the workings of the human body, Annabelle had returned, her face red with outrage.

'All that the newspapers reported was that the women threw rocks at that building, which incidentally was a Government office of some sort,' she hissed. 'They also said that they were arrested, and got a month in a place called Holloway. It made no mention whatsoever of them being flattened by police horses, then pulled back upright by their hair, nor was there any reference to bobbies beating other women with their clubs.'

'Are you surprised?' Lily asked.

Annabelle shook her head. 'Not really, just disgusted. But I intend to set the record straight.'

She reached into the school bag she'd brought with her, and extracted a notebook and pencil. Then without another word she began writing furiously, while Lily began committing to memory the names of the bones that made up the human skeleton, which she found on the first page of the book she'd selected.

When Annabelle had filled two pages of her notebook, she slid it across to Lily. 'What do you think of that?' she asked.

Lily looked down at what Annabelle had written, then smiled. 'It certainly tells the truth about what we witnessed,' she said, 'but what do you intend to do with it?'

'I'm going to move across to one of those desks where they have pens and inkwells, copy it out in my best handwriting, and send it to a newspaper,' Annabelle told her. 'I've had a look through the ones on that stand, and I think that the *Daily Mail* looks promising, to judge by the lively way in which it reports news items. Wish me luck!'

Three days later, after eagerly grabbing that morning's issue of the *Daily Mail* with the same enthusiasm with which she'd scoured the ones from the previous two days, Annabelle was sitting with a dejected expression. Lily did her best to console her.

'Perhaps they haven't got it yet,' she suggested. 'Or, since it happened almost a week ago now, perhaps it's no longer news. It was *very* well written, so I can't imagine why it wasn't published.'

'They don't want the truth, that's why,' Annabelle concluded with a downturned mouth. 'But I'm not giving up that easily. Anyway, how's your research going?'

'It's fascinating,' Lily replied with a broad smile. 'Did you know that our bodies contain more than two hundred bones?'

'All the more for bobbies armed with clubs to break if they don't agree with your views,' Annabelle muttered sourly. 'Is it lunchtime yet? My tummy's rumbling.'

After a few experiments, they'd found a small Italian café in a nearby side street that served tea in various flavours, along with delightful buns called *maritozzi*. The money given to them for their lunches was more than adequate. The two girls quickly became regular customers, and a favourite with the large, affectionate *proprietaria*, Signora Bianchi. In her broken English she would chatter away to them about their hopes, ambitions and family as she took a break from her kitchen and sat with them.

Several days after Annabelle's failure to get her news story published, she and Lily were seated at their usual table on the pavement halfway down Torrington Place, chatting away to Signora Bianchi, when a distant call caught her attention. She cocked her head to one side in order to make sure that she hadn't misheard, and sure enough she heard it again.

'*Votes for Women*! Support the cause and buy the paper! *Votes for Women*!'

She rose from her seat with apologies to her two companions and looked down the street for the source of the shouting. There was a woman half hidden in a shop doorway, holding out copies of some sort of broadsheet and calling out, '*Votes for Women*!' at regular intervals, sometimes adding, 'Support the cause!' or 'Get the truth from the people who know!'

She scurried up to the woman and looked closely at what she appeared to be selling. It was a four-page broadsheet calling itself *Votes for Women*, and its front-page story was all about the work of the Women's Social and Political Union, and the early lives of its founding members. Annabelle looked more carefully at the woman selling copies from the doorway, because she was far from being the usual street news vender. She appeared to be in her early forties, and she was smartly dressed in a long black coat with a matching hat that was adorned with what looked like feathers. She smiled at Annabelle as she called out yet again, '*Votes for Women*! Only a penny! Get this week's copy here!'

'Is that newspaper published by the people who were involved in that recent business in Whitehall, when they were ridden down and beaten by police officers with clubs?' Annabelle asked.

The woman nodded. 'It certainly is. The Women's Social and Political Union — a most worthy cause. Only a penny, and well worth it.'

Annabelle searched in her bag for a penny left over from her lunch money, and handed it over to the woman, who gave her a copy of the newspaper in exchange.

'Did you say this was *this* week's copy?' Annabelle asked. 'Does this mean that it's published every week?'

'It certainly is,' the woman replied, 'but I need to make myself scarce, if you'll excuse me. A bobby just entered the street down there, and he'll confiscate my papers if I don't get a wriggle on.'

She scuttled off in the opposite direction, and Annabelle returned to the café, clutching her prize and wearing a broad smile.

'What's that?' Lily asked. 'And why are you grinning?'

'I think I just found a suitable home for my news story,' Annabelle replied. 'Come on — I want to get back to the library and start writing.'

*

'These are my friends,' Charlotte told Lucy as they sat on the dusty floorboards of the room in White's Row where Ada Penny conducted her self-defence lessons. 'This is Mabel, and this is Lillian.'

'I have a niece with the same name,' Lucy said as warmly as she could, apprehensive of what might come next.

'Lucy's here because she wants to put her bully of a husband in his place,' Charlotte explained, 'but I thought we might involve her in something even more worthwhile.'

It fell silent, until Mabel asked, 'Can she be trusted?'

'We won't know unless we ask her, will we?' Charlotte replied. 'Lucy, apart from fighting back the next time your husband decides to hurt you, might you also be interested in coming to the rescue of other women, using the lessons you're learning here?'

'Am I being invited to become another teacher like Ada?' Lucy asked guardedly.

'Not exactly,' Charlotte said. 'You have hopefully been taking more than a passing interest in recent protests by women who're trying to persuade our Government that the day is long overdue when women should be allowed to vote for who governs the country, take their own places in the House of Commons, and be allowed entry into those professions that men jealously guard for themselves.'

'I've read something about that in the newspapers, certainly,' Lucy confirmed, to a snort of derision from all three women with whom she was talking.

'The newspapers only report a tiny part of what actually happens at those events,' Charlotte told her. 'They go to great lengths to decry the disruption to traffic, the public disorder and the damage that is sometimes inflicted on public buildings, but they make no mention of the brutality inflicted on women who're doing nothing worse than standing up for their rights. In the most recent incident, for example, two of our members were knocked to the ground by police horses, then hauled back upright by their hair and thrown into paddy wagons. They're currently serving a month each in gaol for what they did, while the police got away with their actions.'

'That doesn't sound very fair,' Lucy agreed, since this seemed to be required of her.

Charlotte nodded. 'Indeed it isn't. So we've formed a group of women who can attend these public meetings and fight back, causing bobbies a good deal of pain and suffering while at the same time defending our friends. We call ourselves "The Bodyguard", and we've already had some limited success. But given the resentment and prejudice that's always displayed by the male-dominated Establishment, the newspapers have already labelled us "Amazons", after that tribe of women in Ancient Greece who fought like men, and often *against* men.'

'It sounds like a very worthy cause,' Lucy conceded.

'One that we'd like *you* to join,' Charlotte encouraged. 'You're exactly the sort of person we need — respectably middle-class, married to a professional man, smartly turned out and ladylike in appearance. The last sort of person a bobby would expect to receive a kick in the testicles from, or a broken arm or something. What do you say?'

'May I be allowed to give it some thought?' Lucy hedged. 'Standing up to my husband is one thing, but slogging it out with police officers is another. If I were to get arrested, my husband would divorce me rather than suffer the professional embarrassment, and I'm far too middle-aged to be able to attract another husband. Before my marriage I was a governess, and I could hardly expect to return to that with no up-to-date references.'

'By all means give it some further thought,' Charlotte said, 'but while you're about it, imagine what society could be like if we acquired equality with men. Then you wouldn't need to worry about being supported financially by someone who thinks of you as a mistress and a baby factory, while treating you like a servant.'

To Lucy's profound relief, at that moment Ada called everyone back for the resumed training, and their conversation ended there. However, there was still some vital additional information that Lucy needed to acquire, so when they were all back on their feet she deliberately took Charlotte's purse and hastily read the name inscribed on the inside. Then she feigned embarrassment and handed it over with apologies. 'In the half-light I thought it was mine,' she explained. Charlotte gave her a searching look, but nevertheless appeared to accept her explanation.

As they left the building, Lucy found Percy in a neighbouring shop doorway, sheltering from the wind and puffing on his pipe. She hastily grabbed his arm and began to steer him down the street.

'Get me away from here quickly!' she urged him. 'There is indeed a mob of women fighters. They're called "Amazons" by the newspapers, and I can give you the name "Charlotte Springer". But that's it, Uncle Percy — don't expect me to go back there ever again!'

# CHAPTER SEVEN

'Is that the best you could manage after all this time?' Melville demanded.

Percy swallowed an angry response, opting instead for sullen silence. He'd reluctantly concluded that it was time he reported such progress as he'd made, so had telephoned the house in Tufnell Park Road and requested that a coach collect him from home. He was now in Melville's office, and grinding his teeth in an effort to keep it polite.

'You can hardly write off my efforts thus far as a total failure,' he insisted. 'We — or rather *I* — have confirmed that these "Amazon" women exist, and I have not only located the woman who's training them, but can give you at least one name: Charlotte Springer. That's hardly a total lack of progress.'

'But your niece is refusing to take the matter further?'

'Yes, she is,' Percy conceded, 'and you can hardly blame her for that. From what she's told me about the dreadful things that these women are being trained to do, one would not wish to get the wrong side of them, and Lucy has a husband and four children to think about. These women she's been mixing with are capable of killing with just their umbrellas, for God's sake.'

'Then you must either find another spy who can continue where your niece left off, or somehow infiltrate the group in person, and somehow I can't imagine you in a skirt and blouse. The moustache would obviously have to go, for one thing.'

'What about this Charlotte Springer woman?'

'What about her?'

'Well, if I can locate her — or if you can do that for me — I could keep watch on her. She's obviously part of a larger group; perhaps they meet up secretly somewhere. Then there's that house in White's Row — you could have that raided.'

'And let them know that we're onto them?' Melville retorted. 'You know how these things work, Percy. It's just like brothels, molly houses or illegal prize fights — you close down one place where they meet, and by the following night they've reopened somewhere else.'

'Can you not at least locate Charlotte Springer for me?'

'There are probably at least twenty of those in the Greater London area,' Melville objected.

Percy nodded. 'Give me the list when you've got it, and let me narrow it down to one.'

'Very well, but don't waste any more time. It's probably only a matter of weeks before there's another outrage, and I need these "Amazon" types identified and taken out of circulation. Now it's time for my lunch, and since you don't deserve any, it'll be a table for one. You can also show yourself out.'

'Is there someone here called Annabelle Pickering?' the desk clerk called out softly, and Annabelle looked up quickly from what she'd been writing. There was a woman standing at the front desk who looked like a successful shopkeeper, or perhaps a hospital matron on her day off, and she was gazing hopefully out at the twenty or so readers seated at various desks around the room.

Annabelle raised her hand. 'I'm Annabelle Pickering,' she said.

'This lady's asking for you,' the clerk replied. 'If there's going to be a lengthy conversation, please take it outside.'

'I'll be back in time for lunch,' Annabelle promised Lily as she slid from her chair and walked over to the woman, who smiled at her.

'Would you care for a cup of tea?' she asked. 'There's a delightful tea house just down the street in Bedford Square, and we can talk freely there at one of their outside tables.'

Intrigued, Annabelle followed the lady to the establishment in question, and once she'd ordered tea and muffins for two she looked at Annabelle in a kindly manner that reminded her of Aunt Esther. 'So much talent in someone so young,' she murmured. 'Forgive my manners — I haven't even introduced myself. My name's Emmeline.'

'Emmeline *Pankhurst*?' Annabelle asked in awe.

Her host chuckled before replying, 'No-one so important, I'm afraid. My full name's Emmeline Pethick-Lawrence, which is a bit of a mouthful, so I just use my first name for short. I'm the editor of *Votes for Women*, and after reading that news item you sent to us, I was keen to meet you. It was clearly written on school exercise paper, and yet the prose style was so adult that I was intrigued.'

'Thank you,' Annabelle replied hesitantly, not sure if she was being paid a compliment. 'Do you intend to include my story in one of your weekly editions, or is it too long after the event now?'

'It's *never* too late to bring to public attention the brutal way in which our crusader colleagues are handled by the police, so of *course* we'll be publishing your story, and others like it, if you'd care to carry on covering these events for us.'

'I'd be delighted!' Annabelle enthused, hardly able to believe her ears. 'I've *always* wanted to be a writer, and to get something published is like — well, a dream come true.'

'Did you send any other stories to other newspapers?' Emmeline asked.

Annabelle nodded. 'Just the *Daily Mail*, and when they didn't publish it I got discouraged. But your offer has really perked me up again, and I'll write as many stories as you need.'

'You realise that it will mean you attending more of these rallies, protests and so on?'

'How else could I accurately relate what goes on?'

'Well, as you obviously saw during that attack on the Board of Trade Building, the police can get *very* brutal, and there would always be the risk that you yourself would be manhandled.'

'I'll take that risk,' Annabelle insisted.

'You're very brave, and obviously very committed to our cause,' Emmeline said approvingly.

Annabelle frowned. 'It's more a case that I'm very keen to have stories published, if I'm to be perfectly honest with you. But I certainly *am* determined that everyone should know how those bobbies treat women.'

'That's good enough for us,' Emmeline assured her. 'But with regard to having your stories published, have you ever heard of a newspaper called *The Clarion*?'

'I think I saw one on the paper rack inside the library, but I was too busy reading the *Daily Mail* and the *Illustrated London News* to give it any serious attention.'

'Well, they often take stories from us,' Emmeline told her. 'It's a very progressive newspaper, founded some twenty years ago in order to promote what they call "Socialist" causes, and they've adopted ours. As a matter of interest, when you sent your piece to the *Daily Mail*, did you use your real name?'

'Of course, why?'

Emmeline gave a knowing chuckle. 'That was almost certainly the reason why it never got published, despite its obvious literary merit. The newspapers are just as much a male-dominated world as the professions, and they'd never publish anything written by a woman. We don't want even *The Clarion* to reject your story for that reason, even though it employs some women on its editorial staff. More to the point, to give your items more credibility, should they be cited in the *Daily Mail* or wherever, you need to adopt a nom-de-plume. Do you know what one of those is?'

'I believe that it's an assumed name,' Annabelle replied as her face fell slightly. 'Does that mean I won't get the credit for what I've written?'

'In one sense, yes,' Emmeline conceded, 'but you and I will know who you really are, and you'll have the satisfaction of seeing your work in print. And there's another good reason why I'd recommend it. There may come a point when the authorities start persecuting those of us who publish, or even write, articles that criticise the Government or its agencies. You'll be accusing the police of criminal offences, and we don't want you prosecuted for treason, or sedition, or something like that.'

'I think I should tell you that I'm sort of adopted,' Annabelle admitted, 'and that my adoptive father is a senior police officer at Scotland Yard. Does that change your mind about publishing my stories?'

'No, it just makes me appreciate your honesty and courage. Now, what sort of name shall we give you?'

'Something fairly close to my real name, if possible,' Annabelle replied. 'Perhaps "Anthony Pickford", or something like that?'

'Excellent!' Emmeline replied. 'Now, would Anthony Pickford like to write another story — *before* the events described in it actually occur?'

'Oh yes, that sounds very exciting,' Annabelle replied.

Emmeline frowned. 'Exciting, perhaps, but not very edifying. Have you been following what happened to those two women who were arrested for chucking rocks at the Board of Trade Building?'

'Not really, although I remember their names from the newspaper report of their court appearance. They're called Ada Wright and Sarah Carwin, from memory, and they got a month each, to be served in somewhere called Holloway.'

'That's a prison in north London,' Emmeline told her, 'and they both tried to claim what's called "political status". This means that they get better conditions inside the prison, and they both claimed, quite rightly, that they were only in prison because they'd been advocating for a political cause. They were refused, on the grounds that they'd been sentenced for what the authorities called "malicious damage", so they broke every window in their cells in protest. Then, when they were put on a bread-and-water diet as a punishment, they refused to consume even that, and they've embarked on something called a "hunger strike". That's what I want you to write about. That and the story of Marion Dunlop, whose actions they're imitating.'

'Tell me about Marion Dunlop first,' Annabelle urged her.

'I will after I've ordered more tea, since this conversation is turning out to be longer, and more thirst-making, than I'd anticipated.'

Once the waitress had deposited another pot of tea on their table, Emmeline went on, 'Now then, Marion Dunlop. She's been one of our more active campaigners for some years, and she's also in Holloway Gaol at the moment, this time for something she wrote on the wall of the House of Commons. She went inside only days after Ada and Sarah, and while I'm not sure if they've been allowed to communicate with each other, they've all three agreed on this policy that Marion adopted from the very first day of her confinement, when told that she wouldn't be getting "political status". As I already mentioned, it's something called a "hunger strike", which is precisely what it sounds like.'

'You mean that they refuse to eat anything?' Annabelle asked, horrified.

'Or drink anything, either,' Emmeline added.

Annabelle thought about it for a moment. 'They intend to die in prison, then?'

'Of *course* they don't,' Emmeline insisted. 'But they're assuming that the governor of Holloway, who incidentally is a woman, wouldn't want the bad publicity that would attend the death by starvation of three of her inmates. So Marion, Ada and Sarah hope that by this means they'll strike a blow for all other Suffragists who should be allowed political status inside the prison.'

'And what if the governor *doesn't* relent?'

'Then they'll become our first martyrs to the cause,' Emmeline replied with a grim expression.

'But that's *awful*!' Annabelle gasped. 'Dying in that horrible way, just to make a point about the conditions they're being kept in.'

'Not just them, but all future Suffragists,' Emmeline reminded her. 'It's a worthy cause, but no-one will know anything about it unless you write that story, and as soon as possible. If you could send it to this address, I'll have it set into type ahead of next week's edition.'

She handed Annabelle a business card on which was written an address on the Strand. Annabelle tucked it into the top pocket of her tunic as she rose and thanked Emmeline again, both for the tea and the opportunity to realise her ambition to write news items for publication. Then she hurried back down to the library, where a pouting Lily was seated in her usual place.

'I couldn't wait any longer for lunch, so I went without you,' she complained. 'Signora Bianchi was most put out.'

'I was given something to eat by that lady who came here to speak with me,' Annabelle replied, 'and just *wait* until I tell you my news! It'll have to wait until we walk back to the station to meet your father, but there's something I need you to do for me this afternoon.'

'What's that?'

'Find out how long the human body can survive without food or water.'

The urgent meeting of the Cabinet had been called for one specific purpose, and Prime Minister Asquith handed the chair over to Home Secretary Herbert Gladstone as soon as everyone was seated.

'It's a tricky one,' Gladstone admitted. 'Three of these damned self-proclaimed champions of women's rights are demanding political status, and have gone on hunger strike until they get it.'

'Let them starve themselves to death, then,' Lord Chancellor Loreburn suggested gleefully, to a frown from Gladstone.

'It's gone beyond that, I'm afraid,' he told those around the table.

'You mean they're already dead?' Loreburn asked hopefully, but Gladstone shook his head.

'No — they've been released by the Governor of Holloway, who was fearful that she'd be accused of manslaughter if they were allowed to commit suicide on her watch. They're now being feted as heroines, and paraded up and down the streets.'

'Manslaughter would have been a debateable charge, legally speaking,' observed Loreburn, a former judge with a stellar legal career behind him, 'but if they've been released, what's your problem?'

'Others will follow their example,' Gladstone replied. 'The word's obviously out that you can get out of gaol simply by going on hunger strike, and we need some means of preventing that.'

'Give in to their demands, and classify them as political prisoners, you mean?' Loreburn responded. 'How can their offences be considered "political" in nature, when they consist of smashing windows, defacing public buildings and fighting with police officers?'

'They can't, clearly,' Gladstone conceded, 'but I have something more suitable in mind. I've outlined my idea to Bertie, and he's in agreement in principle.'

Asquith nodded his confirmation, and Gladstone continued.

'If they won't eat voluntarily, then we force them to.'

'Is that physically possible?' asked Edward Grey, Foreign Secretary.

Gladstone nodded. 'So I'm told by the various medical experts I've consulted. What I need from you is your support for the necessary orders being passed down to prison governors. Holloway primarily, obviously, but other prisons as well, in case other types of offender latch on to the idea. It got a lot of newspaper coverage.'

'Do it, and let's go home,' Loreburn suggested, and ten minutes later the Cabinet room was once again empty.

*

'Would you like to meet Marion Dunlop?' Emmeline Pethick-Lawrence asked Annabelle as they met by arrangement in the same open-air I in Bedford Square. 'She wants to thank you for your efforts in persuading the Holloway governor to release her and the other two, and she has something else she wants to bring to your attention for possible publication.'

'I'm sure you're exaggerating my influence,' Annabelle replied modestly.

Emmeline shook her head vigorously. 'Definitely not, young lady. You wield a powerful pen, and when you described in horrible detail what death by starvation must feel like, it stirred many a heart. More to the point, perhaps, it shook even the editor of the *Daily Mail*, and he's asked for more contributions from Anthony Pickford, who I described as a journalist new to our shores from South Africa who's eager to make a name for himself over here.'

'When can I meet Marion?' Annabelle asked.

Emmeline nodded into the far distance. 'She's over there on that bench, pretending to feed squirrels and awaiting my signal.'

She waved her hand, and the smartly dressed, thin-faced lady waved back, then came over. While Emmeline set about ordering more tea and muffins, and an extra teacup, Marion grasped Annabelle by both hands and looked into her eyes.

'So *you're* the young lady to whom I owe my freedom!' she enthused. 'I hadn't expected someone so young, but thank you a thousand times.'

'I was just trying to persuade Emmeline that my humble efforts are at risk of being over-valued,' Annabelle said, blushing. 'You should really thank my sort of adopted sister, who did all the research using medical books that enabled me to describe death by slow starvation.'

'But without your talent with words, that information would just have remained in some dry, dusty medical tome. And I wish you to employ those talents again.'

'She hardly needs any encouragement,' Emmeline said with a chuckle, as the waitress took off with her order, 'although she may not find the subject matter very pleasant to put into her own words.'

'It can't be any more of a challenge than describing a slow death,' Annabelle replied, 'so what is it this time?'

'Sexual abuse of female prisoners,' Marion replied bluntly, looking closely at Annabelle's face for any reaction.

'In prison? Did this happen to you?' she asked.

'No, not me. It happened to Ada and Sarah, while they were in Bow Street police station, awaiting their appearance before the magistrate the following morning. Two police officers entered each of their cells in turn and took sexual liberties with them. Not rape, but as good as.'

'They had a cell each?' Annabelle queried. 'I thought it was part of the awful conditions to which Suffragists are subjected that they be herded together, ten to a cell intended for only one.'

Marion nodded. 'That's what makes the matter even more outrageous. They were deliberately isolated in order to allow the assaults to take place, which means that those in authority inside the police station must have been complicit.'

'So much for the so-called matrons,' Emmeline said with a snort, and when Annabelle looked puzzled, she added, 'Have you not heard about the alleged matron system?'

'I can't say I have,' Annabelle admitted.

'In order to forestall any allegations of female prisoners being misused in any way by constables, the various police stations in which they're being held have appointed women to guard their interests and preserve their modesty and virtue,' Emmeline explained. 'These women are called "matrons", and the public are encouraged to believe that there's no risk of *precisely* what Marion just described.'

'So you can plainly see why we need you to expose the truth,' Marion added.

'Of course I will, if you can give me a little more detail,' Annabelle assured them. 'Then could I ask a favour for my adopted sister Lily?'

'What's that?'

'Well, like me she was present at that dreadful business when Ada and Sarah were arrested, and she helped to tend to some of those who were so brutally injured by bobbies. She's making a study of medicine at a local library — the one in which Emmeline found me — and she's anxious to meet up again with the woman she assisted on that occasion. She was wearing some sort of sash describing her as a "medical orderly", and her name was Sarah Millichip.'

'I know Sarah very well,' Emmeline said, 'so when we next meet, bring this sister of yours along with you, and I'll bring Sarah.'

'I'll be sure to do that,' Annabelle promised, 'since apart from anything else, it'll mean that I'm not the only one going behind our parents' backs.'

# CHAPTER EIGHT

'What have you been up to now?' Beattie demanded as Percy walked through the scullery door and carefully removed his gardening boots, as per the standing orders that prevailed in the Hackney house.

'Weeding between my potato rows, why?' Percy asked. 'Have I in some way contravened a new Beatrice Enright Statute of which I was not even aware?'

'If it weren't for me laying down a few basic rules as to how this house is to be managed, it would look like an East End dwelling of ill repute,' she countered frostily. 'But my enquiry is more to do with *this*,' she added as she produced an envelope from the folds of her kitchen apron. 'It arrived by second post while you were hiding in the garden, and it looks very official. Have you been summonsed or something?'

Percy took the envelope from her and ripped it open after noting the official crest with which it was adorned. Inside was a single typewritten sheet of names, and he cursed quietly — but not quietly enough to avoid a soft tut from Beattie as she adjusted her apron and took herself off to the sitting room to renew her daily battle with the dust.

There were, seemingly, nine women in the Greater London area who had the name Charlotte Springer, and Percy was presumably expected to discover which one had offered Lucy the opportunity to become an Amazon for the Suffragette cause. Their addresses ranged from Bermondsey, south of the river, to Finchley on its northern perimeter, and it would take him days, if not weeks, of patient, stealthy enquiry to learn which one required the attention of MO5.

He sat down heavily at the kitchen table, took out his pipe, remembered that smoking in the house was designated as one of the Seven Deadly Sins of 37 Victoria Park Road, Hackney, and took himself back out to his garden shed. Then, as the acrid fumes of his favourite tobacco blocked his view beyond the small window that faced his vegetable patch, he smiled and formulated a challenge for Beattie. *If smoking is such a sin, how come my favourite tobacco is named after Saint Bruno?*

Pleased by his own wit, he came back to the more immediate problem that currently clouded his horizon. How could he best determine, without a great deal of legwork and undercover intrigue, which of the nine ladies called Charlotte Springer was the one who could lead Melville and his pack of hounds to the Amazons responsible for stealing explosives?

His memory drifted back to the grubby premises in White's Court to which he'd taken Lucy, and her blank refusal to assist further. Then he remembered something else, and with crossed fingers he left the garden shed to make an eager trip to the telephone.

'Don't bring that awful thing in here!' Beattie yelled as he walked back into the scullery with his pipe still going like a recently lit bonfire. He walked back outside, placed the pipe on the outside window ledge in the hope that it would still be there on his return, then walked to the telephone desk in the hall.

Lucy answered on the third ring, and Percy wasted little time after the introductory mutual enquiries regarding health.

'That woman you were with on that first night you were learning self-defence down in Spitalfields — was that Charlotte Springer?'

'Yes, why?'

'Just that you've saved me a good deal of potential hard work. Did she by any chance say where she lived?'

'No — only that she needed to get a cab home afterwards. And from memory, she said that in your hearing as well.'

'Yes, she did, and that's just given me a *very* good idea.'

'I hope it doesn't involve me again.'

'No, it doesn't — not yet, anyway.'

'Well, forgive me if I put this telephone down before it does. Good morning, Uncle Percy.'

'You *really* caught the attention of the editor of the *Daily Mail* *this* time,' Emmeline said with a grin as she poured them all tea and pushed the muffin plate in Annabelle's direction. 'And it's good to meet your sister as well — hopefully Sarah will be here in a short while, only she has to travel from Fulham to join us.'

They were meeting again at the café in Bedford Square of which they had become regular patrons of late, and this time Annabelle had brought Lily with her. It was close to the middle of the day, and both girls had slunk out of the library where they were supposed to be studying.

'Do you really think it's going to make a difference?' Annabelle asked eagerly.

Emmeline nodded. 'The allegation that two women were sexually molested while supposedly in the safety of a police cell really caused a storm, it seems. I heard two women talking about it in scandalised tones as I sat near them on the omnibus on my way into the office this morning, and then I got a telephone call from a friend on the *Daily Mail* — female, of course, although in a minor office capacity. It seems that several other women have contacted the paper with similar allegations, and the editor has commissioned an enquiry box in tomorrow's edition, asking for women with similar experiences to contact them. Well done, Annabelle!'

'I can't honestly claim to have enjoyed writing about it,' Annabelle said, shuddering, 'and I can't imagine how I'd feel if it happened to me.'

'Well, hopefully you won't need to find out,' Emmeline replied, then directed a broad smile over Annabelle's shoulder. 'That looks like Sarah now, making her way down between the rose displays.'

'I was hoping it was you!' Sarah Millichip beamed as she was formally introduced to Lily. 'You showed such great promise when we were doing what we could for those poor women in Horse Guards Avenue, and the more I can recruit into my little band, the better. I forgot your name in all that excitement, I'm afraid.'

'That's because my aunt dragged me away,' Lily explained, 'and I've been studying medical books in a local library since then. I'd really like to become a nurse one day.'

'No better training than learning on the job,' Sarah told her as she nodded her thanks for the cup of tea that Emmeline had just poured for her.

Emmeline then introduced Annabelle. 'This is the remarkably talented young lady who wrote that story about the outrages inflicted on Ada and Sarah inside Bow Street police station — the story accredited to "Anthony Pickford". Meet Anthony Pickford in the flesh.'

'A wonderful effort, young lady,' Sarah enthused as she shook Annabelle's hand. 'I hope you'll be on hand on the eighteenth of next month.'

'More fights with police officers?' Annabelle asked nervously.

Sarah shook her head. 'Something *much* more newsworthy — a full scale invasion of the House of Commons!'

'So you won't need me?' Lily asked with a look of disappointment.

Sarah chuckled. 'Did I say that? What do you think will be the likely reaction when our sisters bomb the House with leaflets from the gallery, and heckle the Prime Minister during debates? They'll most likely be thrown bodily out of the chamber, resulting in a few broken limbs, which will give you some valuable experience in bone-setting.'

'You'll certainly need me there, with my pencil and notebook,' Annabelle said, then her face fell as she asked, 'What day of the week will that be?'

'Friday,' Sarah replied. 'There's bound to be a full house, because they'll be debating a proposed new Licensing Bill, and every member has been left in no doubt by their constituents which way they want the vote to go. Our friends are planning on occupying the Ladies Gallery, then causing as much disruption as they can.'

'I'll *definitely* be there,' Annabelle confirmed.

'So will I,' Lily added, 'and we can both be there in secret because our parents will think that we're studying in the library. Will you need me inside, as well as Annabelle?'

'No,' Sarah replied. 'We'll wait outside until they start throwing our members out onto the ground in front of the main entrance to the House, which I believe is called Cromwell Green. That's when they'll need us to do running repairs to their injuries.'

'It sounds as if it'll be a lot of fun,' Annabelle mused, then felt instantly regretful as she saw Sarah's face darken.

'There's nothing "fun" about any of this, young lady, as your sister will no doubt tell you when she's finished dealing with blood and broken bones,' she admonished her. 'Make sure that your eventual story reflects the full horror and degradation of it, that's all.'

The cabbie whose coach was drawn up at the corner of Crispin Street and White's Row was having a very slow night. Tuesdays were never particularly busy, and it had just started to rain. Added to that was the fact that he was obliged to tout unofficially for business in a very insalubrious area of the East End because he'd recently been denied a renewal of his licence, due to a misunderstanding regarding the precise professions of some of his regular lady customers. So all in all, he was delighted when the smartly dressed gentleman offered him a good sum for simply taking his cab into White's Row and following his instructions as they rolled slowly down it.

'That lady in the long green coat, and the hat with dead birds all over it,' came the instruction from the passenger, before he ducked down out of sight below the window. 'And remember what to ask her.'

As the coach pulled slowly towards the group of women who'd just left the nondescript building with the boarded-up windows, one of them put out a hand and called for the cab to stop for her. It was the woman indicated by his passenger, so the cabbie asked, 'Where to, Missus?'

'Finchley. Regent's Park Road, to be precise.'

'Sorry, I doesn't go that far at this time o' night,' the cabbie replied as he pulled away from the side of the street, leaving an outraged Charlotte Springer standing with an open mouth.

'All right, guv'nor?' the cabbie asked once they'd reached the end of the street.

'Perfect, thank you,' Percy confirmed as he alighted from the coach, relieved that he now only had to investigate the activities of one of the ladies whose addresses had come from Melville.

'Have you seen all this rubbish in the papers?' Chief Superintendent Barrymore demanded from Jack's office doorway, brandishing various copies of the offending publications.

'What rubbish, and what papers?' Jack asked listlessly. Barrymore was easily affronted by anything in the dailies that reflected badly on the Met.

'The bloody *Daily Mail*, for a start,' Barrymore raged. 'According to what it's been publishing these past few days, women confined to cells within the Met are at risk of being sexually molested.'

'And?' Jack asked.

'And I want you to find out where all this balderdash is coming from, that's what.'

'Why me in particular, sir?'

'Because if it's true, then it's obviously a disciplinary matter, and you're head of Manpower, that's why.'

'I thought you'd discounted it as "balderdash",' Jack reminded him.

Barrymore's face reddened. 'Just find out if it's true, then report back to me either way.'

'Yes, sir. Might I know which police stations have been named?'

'Several, as it transpires, all in connection with that Suffragette nonsense, which is why I'm more inclined to disbelieve it. But begin with Bow Street, since there were specific names mentioned in connection with the alleged victims. It's all in here,' he added as he walked further into the office and slapped a recent copy of the *Daily Mail* down on

Jack's desk, before marching back out again and disappearing from sight.

Jack sighed heavily, then called for his sergeant, who occupied a desk in the hallway outside, and had no doubt heard the entire conversation.

'Rearrange my recruitment interviews for the next few days, and tell Bow Street to expect me in the morning,' he instructed.

By ten o'clock the following morning, Jack was seated in front of the desk occupied by Inspector Archie Montford, the senior officer who ran the very busy Bow Street police station, and reading from the notes he'd made the previous afternoon.

'According to my information,' he told Montford, 'two ladies, Ada Wright and Sarah Carwin, were brought in here on the afternoon of the twenty-ninth of June last, accused of offences arising from a Suffragette outrage in Whitehall. I'm commanded by Chief Superintendent Barrymore, my ultimate superior in the Met, to enquire as to what happened to them from that time until their appearance before the duty magistrate the following morning.'

'They would have been processed at the Charge Bar in the normal way, then allocated a cell — probably together, because we were very busy that day, on account of that business you referred to outside the Board of Trade Building. They would then have been fed sometime later that evening, and again the following morning, before being taken upstairs to be processed through court by the magistrate. As you probably know, it's all dealt with in the same building here.'

Jack frowned. 'I don't wish to know what "would have" happened, had normal procedures been observed. I need to know precisely what *did* happen. For example, according to an account that was published in the *Daily Mail*, written by some guttersnipe news reporter who claims to have got the information first-hand, the two ladies were allocated a cell each. From what you just said, this was highly unlikely, so were they, or were they not?'

'I'll need to consult the cell records,' Montford hedged.

'I can wait,' Jack said firmly.

Ten minutes later the records were on the inspector's desk, and he nodded before sliding them over for Jack to read. 'As you can see,' he said, 'they were consigned four to a cell that night, in cells normally accommodating only two at a time. As I already mentioned, we were over capacity due to the unusually high number of arrests. Ada Wright and Sarah Carwin were in a cell along with Mary Blatchford and Elizabeth Brady, two fellow Suffragettes.'

'So the *Daily Mail* got that wrong, at least,' Jack replied. 'As a matter of interest, were you on duty that evening?'

'Eventually,' Montford confirmed. 'I was supposed to be rostered off, but such was the chaos in here after the outrage down the road that the desk sergeant requested that I be called back on duty. I got here at about eight o'clock that evening, made sure that everything was in order, then went home for a few hours' sleep before coming back on at eight the next morning in order to supervise the orderly transfer of prisoners upstairs.'

'So whatever may have happened in here prior to eight o'clock on the evening of the twenty-ninth of June occurred before you arrived?' Jack asked.

Montford nodded. 'Obviously, although had there been some incident that I needed to know about, it would have been reported to me on my arrival, but nothing was.'

'Who would have been in charge of the cell allocation that evening?'

'Initially, the desk sergeant at the Charge Bar; then he would hand the prisoners over to the senior turnkey, to be taken down to the cells to which they'd been allocated.'

'And after that?'

'I'm not sure what you mean,' Montford said with a frown.

'If for some reason there was a need to rearrange the cell allocations — for example, if one prisoner took offence at something said by another, and it was necessary to separate them — who would have seen to that?'

'One of the turnkeys, obviously, probably on the authority of the senior turnkey, but these cell records don't appear to record any such need.'

Jack looked more closely at the cell records, then sought clarification. 'I see that you have two cell corridors, one above the other. The ground-level corridor has cells numbered eleven to seventeen, while the lower level houses twenty-one to twenty-seven. Would I be correct in concluding from those numbers that you have six cells on each level, with a total notional capacity for housing twenty-four prisoners?'

'Correct, although as I already mentioned, we had four to a cell in some cases, due to the high numbers of arrests. One of those cells contained the two women you're enquiring about — Wright and Carwin — along with two others, Blatchford and Brady. All of them were involved in that shameful business in Whitehall.'

'I assume that your turnkeys are civilians, in accordance with the usual arrangement?' Jack asked.

'Of course.'

'Only, I notice that while the senior turnkey for that evening was one Thomas Johns, the one working under his supervision was named Ethel Merriman,' Jack continued. 'Is that a clerical error, or do you employ female turnkeys?'

'In a sense, yes, we do,' Montford confirmed. 'Are you familiar with the matron system?'

'I've heard of it, certainly,' Jack said. 'Civilian women employed to guard the interests of female prisoners?'

'Correct, which is why Ethel Merriman was carrying out turnkey duties that evening. We find it more convenient, and less expensive, to combine the two duties.'

'And how would she have been recruited?'

'I have no idea, specifically,' Montford said, 'but they're usually nominated by uniformed officers allocated to this station; they're frequently their wives or other female relatives or friends. We have a Constable Merriman allocated to Bow Street, so I assume that this woman Ethel is related to him in some way.'

'Would it be possible for me to speak with her?'

'Not immediately, obviously, but I can have her brought in later today, if that would be convenient.'

'Yes, please do,' Jack requested. 'I notice that by the following morning there was another turnkey on duty, charged with conveying the prisoners up to the courtroom. Daniel Cropper?'

'Quite possibly. The allocation of turnkey duties is the desk sergeant's responsibility, and I can't be expected to be on top of all the points of detail. But if you want to speak to him as well, it can be arranged, although it's turning into a very busy day for you.'

'*All* my days are busy,' Jack said, smiling back wanly, 'and I'd rather get this matter resolved quickly, without the need to travel backwards and forwards from the Yard. So thank you for your time so far, and if you could line up those two turnkeys for me to interview later today, I'll go upstairs and speak to the court clerk.'

As he sat in the deserted courtroom upstairs, waiting for the clerk to bring the relevant records for the morning of the thirtieth of June, in case either Ada Wright or Sarah Carwin had made a formal complaint regarding their treatment, Jack pondered over the notes he'd taken while interviewing Inspector Montford. The inspector struck him as all too casual and unconcerned regarding a serious allegation that had the potential to reflect very badly on the way in which he discharged his duties. At the same time, Jack refreshed his memory of the names of those who'd been allocated to the cells below.

This proved to be very fortuitous a few minutes later, when the clerk reappeared with the court record for the thirtieth of June, with apologies for the delay. 'As it turns out,' the clerk told him, 'it was quite an intense morning, with those newspaper types all over the place, given what those two women were charged with. Fortunately, there weren't too many other matters on the list that day.'

Something jarred inside Jack's brain, as he tried to reconcile what he'd just heard with the description given by Inspector Montford of a hectic night involving overcrowded cells and an unusually high number of prisoners. Something didn't ring true, and instinctively he carefully examined the court records that he'd just been handed.

His instinct had been correct. There was no reference to either a Mary Blatchford or an Elizabeth Brady appearing in Bow Street Magistrates' Court that morning. Someone upstairs had a good deal of explaining to do.

# CHAPTER NINE

'I 'opes as 'ow there's nowt wrong wiv the way I bin doin' me duties,' Daniel Cropper murmured as he sat nervously in front of the desk behind which Jack sat, in a borrowed office, enquiring into events on a morning when he'd been on duty.

'That remains to be seen,' Jack replied ominously, a veteran of disciplinary hearings, 'so tell me what you recall about the morning of the thirtieth of June last.'

'Were that when them Suffragist women come through?'

'They're called Suffragettes, but yes — those,' Jack confirmed.

'I remembers that pretty well,' Cropper told him, 'on account o' the fact that the street outside were full of all them newspaper types, shoutin' an' carryin' on out the front of the buildin', an' 'alf a dozen bobbies barrin' the door to 'em. We 'ad ter all but smuggle them two up inter the courtroom. I just pulled 'em out a the cell they was in, then took 'em upstairs, proper smartish like.'

'Leaving the other two in the cell?' Jack prompted him.

Cropper looked confused. '*What* other two, sir?'

'I was told that Cell Twelve had four women in it that night,' Jack replied.

'No, sir, only them two — them Suffragists, like I said.'

'So after you'd taken them up to the courtroom, what did you do next?'

'Stayed wiv' 'em, sir, 'til the beak told me ter take 'em back down again. Then I brought the other four up.'

'What other four was that?'

'Them what were left fer the beak ter deal wiv — Cells Thirteen an' Fourteen, two apiece. From memory, them in Thirteen was two blokes in fer thievin', and them in Fourteen was totties pulled in during the night shift.'

'So in total that morning, there were only six prisoners taken up into the courtroom, and only two of those were Suffragettes. Have I got that right?'

'As best as I remember it, yeah, that's right. 'Ave I done sumfin' wrong?'

'No, far from it,' Jack assured him, 'but it was suggested to me that the night of the twenty-ninth into the thirtieth was a very busy one, with all the cells full, and in places overcrowded.'

'Wiv respect, sir, someone's bin feedin' yer a load o' rubbish. It were pretty quiet — or at least, it woulda bin, 'ad all them newspaper folk not bin creatin' such a disturbance. The beak ordered 'em all out of 'is court in the end.'

'And the only cells occupied that night were Numbers Twelve, Thirteen and Fourteen?'

'Yeah, that's right. None of 'em on the lower level — just them three on the ground floor.'

'Thank you, Mr Cropper,' Jack said with a smile. 'You've been a great help to my enquiry, and let me assure you that there's no suggestion of any dereliction of duty on your part.'

'Well, that's a relief,' said Cropper, sighing heavily as he rose to leave. 'An' thank yer fer bein' so polite an' all — it ain't everyone around 'ere what's like that.'

Next in was Ethel Merriman. Armed with what he knew already, Jack decided to set her a simple trap.

'It's "Mrs" Merriman, is it?' he asked politely, hoping to establish a false sense of security.

'That's right, sir,' she confirmed. 'Me 'usband's Jack Merriman, what normally does the Covent Garden beat.'

'And it was your husband who got you the job as a matron?'

'Yeah, that's right. There's nowt 'under'anded about that, yer understand? A few of the wives does matron duties around 'ere.'

'No-one's suggesting that, Mrs Merriman, so don't worry. But I'm not all that familiar with how the system works, since I'm from Scotland Yard, and we don't have matrons there. What do the duties involve?'

'Just lookin' after women what's brought in 'ere after bein' arrested. Totties, fer the most part, an' a few shoplifters and drunks.'

'And Suffragettes?'

'Yeah, we gets a few o' them in 'ere, on account of Parliament an' Whitehall bein' on our patch. They likes ter cause trouble around places like that.'

'And on the twenty-ninth of June last, you were on duty when two women were brought in, accused of throwing rocks at a Government building in Whitehall,' Jack prompted her. 'I don't expect you to remember their names, but do you remember the occasion?'

'Yeah, plain as yesterday,' she said, ''cos they was goin' on about 'avin' bin roughed up by them bobbies what brought 'em in. From the Westminster lot, as I recall — them what rides 'orses.'

'And where were they when you first saw them?'

'In a cell, they was, wiv two others. One o' the fust ones as yer go in along the ground floor level.'

'Could it have been Cell Twelve?'

'Yeah, most likely. Like I said — one of the fust 'uns in there.'

‘And there were two other women in there with them?’

‘Yeah, four ter the cell. It were a bit crowded that night, see, on account of all them arrests that afternoon.’

‘Suffragettes?’

‘Most likely.’

‘And what time did you go off duty that evening?’

‘Musta bin around midnight or so.’

‘And in all the time you were on duty, did any of the four women in Cell Twelve get transferred to another cell?’

‘Nah, don’t fink so, anyroad.’

‘And did anyone from that cell complain of being ill-treated?’

‘Nah, definitely not.’

It was now time to deliver the first blow. Jack stared directly into her eyes as he asked, ‘How did the other two women manage to escape while you were supposed to be supervising them?’

‘Beg yours?’

‘According to Daniel Cropper, who took over from you that night, there were only two women left in that cell when he opened it the following morning. The two Suffragettes, Ada Wright and Sarah Carwin. So where did the other two get to?’

‘I doesn’t know, does I?’ Ethel protested, clearly flustered. ‘They musta already gone up ter the court ahead o’ the other two. I were ’ome in bed.’

‘They didn’t exist, did they?’ Jack challenged her.

Her gaze dropped to the floor. ‘What d’yer mean?’

‘What I just said. According to the cell records, the other two women in Cell Twelve with the two Suffragettes were called Mary Blatchford and Elizabeth Brady. But Daniel Cropper only recalls taking the other two — Wright and Carwin — upstairs into the courtroom, and the court records contain no trace of either Mary Blatchford or Elizabeth Brady. So who forged the cell records, and why?'

'I doesn't know, does I?' Ethel all but wailed. 'I just does my job, an' the last I saw o' them what yer talkin about — them Suffragettes — was when I separated them, like I was asked ter do.'

'You never mentioned that,' Jack said coldly. 'So if you're to avoid serious criminal charges for allowing prisoners in your custody to escape, not to mention dismissal from your matron duties, let's start again, and tell me the truth this time.'

'I only did what I were told ter do,' Ethel pleaded, on the verge of tears.

'Which was what, precisely?' Jack demanded. 'And bear in mind that your honesty at this moment may well improve your prospects.'

'Well, it were like this,' she continued in hushed tones, having first looked behind her to confirm that they were alone, with the door closed. 'I'd not been on duty long when I gets this 'ere message ter transfer one of them women from Cell Twelve inter Cell Eleven. I weren't told why, but I guessed it were 'cos there was lots of spare cells that night, so I just did what I were told.'

'Who gave you that instruction, and which of the women did you transfer?'

'No idea which of them it were, but I just did like I were asked. It were the sergeant out the front what asked me ter do it, an' then when I reported back that it'd been done, I saw two bobbies goin' down inter the cells, where they 'ad no business goin' as far as I knew. That were all, *honest*, but I 'eard later that the two women 'ad bin messed about a bit by a couple of bobbies, and that I were ter keep my mouth shut about what

I'd done, if I knew what were good for me. If asked, I were ter pretend that all the cells was full that night, on both levels.'

'Can you tell me the names of the two uniformed constables who entered the cells after you'd separated the two women?'

'I *could*, but I daresn't — *honest* I daresn't. I bin warned ter keep me trap shut, or I'm a goner.'

Jack thought briefly, then put on his sternest face. 'I intend to make a big issue of this, and certain people will be going to prison for what went on in here. If you don't want to be one of them, you'll have to repeat in court what you just told me, do you understand?'

'If I does, will yer make sure as nobody comes after me?'

'Of course I will, you can be assured of that. And thank you for your courage and honesty so far. You're free to go now, but say nothing of this conversation to anyone.'

It was after five in the evening by the time that Jack returned to the Yard, and when he presented himself in Barrymore's office doorway it was obvious that the Chief Superintendent was preparing to depart for the day.

'It's true, sir!' Jack told him, but his only reward was a stern frown.

'*What's* true, and can't it wait until the morning?' Barrymore demanded.

'It could, but I thought you'd want to know without delay,' Jack persevered. 'Those two Suffragettes who were reported in the newspapers as having been separated and placed in a single cell each, then sexually assaulted? I've just returned from speaking to a woman attached to Bow Street police station, who confirms that she was the one who separated them.'

'But that doesn't prove that they were assaulted, does it?'

'She also saw two constables who she can name entering the cell corridor, where they had no business to be.'

'Again, that proves nothing,' Barrymore insisted, but Jack wasn't finished.

'The cell records for that evening were falsified in order to give the impression that they had more prisoners than they actually did. The cover-up seems to have been at the instigation of the sergeant on the front desk, and was possible because of slack supervision by the inspector in charge at Bow Street.'

'And you're basing all these serious allegations on something you were told by a *woman*?' Barrymore challenged him as he reached for his briefcase and gloves. 'What was a woman doing inside the cell area of a police station in the first place?'

'She's one of those matrons who're appointed to prevent *precisely* that sort of thing from happening! The system is clearly flawed, if not actually rotten, and I intend to undertake further investigations in every police station referred to in that newspaper article you gave me, in case the same thing has been happening there.'

'You'll do no such thing, do you understand?' Barrymore snapped. 'The last thing we need, at this sensitive political time, is a suggestion that women who're arrested and taken into custody for staging demonstrations are subjected to sexual attacks by the very police officers who arrested them in the first place. Imagine what that would do for the public's perception of the Met. Now, if you'll excuse me, I'm in danger of missing my train.'

'You asked me to find out whether or not the rumours about Bow Street were true,' Jack reminded him. 'Why do I suddenly get the feeling that you only intended for me to report back that they were false?'

'That's a scandalous slur on my integrity, Enright, and I'll remind you of who you're talking to. Now get out of my way!'

*

'You're late home,' Esther commented as Jack slammed the front door and threw his hat towards the hat peg, missing it by even more than his usual margin of error. 'By the look on your face, it hasn't been a good day.'

'Get me a whisky,' he demanded, and she recoiled slightly from the tone of his voice as he took off his overcoat, threw it down on the hall carpet and stormed into the living room.

He looked up, shamefaced, as she handed him the whisky with a slightly trembling hand. 'Sorry,' he muttered. 'I shouldn't take it out on you, but, as you guessed, it's been a terrible day altogether.'

'Do you want to talk about it?'

'Do you want to hear?'

'Of course I do, Jack. You listen to my gripes often enough, so it's the least I can do. Just don't bark at me, that's all.'

'I'm really, really sorry about that,' Jack replied as he patted the space next to him on the sofa. 'How would you respond if you'd discovered that female prisoners were being sexually assaulted in the cells of one of our largest and busiest police stations, only to be told to keep your mouth shut about it?'

'Are you serious?' Esther asked in alarm. 'I read something along those lines in one of the daily papers, and I think they mentioned Bow Street. Is it true, then?'

'So it would seem,' Jack confirmed. 'It was those two Suffragettes who were taken in charge after that business in Whitehall that Annabelle and Lily nearly got involved in. The women were put in a cell together inside Bow Street, then separated so that two constables could enter each cell and have their way with them.'

'That's indescribably awful!' Esther replied as some of the colour left her face. 'But aren't there measures in place to prevent that sort of thing? Women installed in police stations to guard their interests?'

'It was just such a woman who confessed to what happened,' Jack replied gloomily. 'The system has clearly failed, if it was ever really intended to work in the first place. The rot begins at the very top, with the inspector in charge not exercising the slightest supervisory control over events in his own station, a corrupt sergeant who's not above forging the cell records, and a so-called matron who was too scared to blow the whistle until I threatened her with criminal charges. But with her testimony, and the court records to confirm that the cell occupation numbers for that night were forged, I think I have enough evidence to prove what actually happened.'

'So why the glum face and bad temper?'

'Because Barrymore — my ultimate superior — as good as ordered me to cover it up! Politics and public image are clearly rated much more highly in the Met than truth and justice.'

'I can see why you're so down, but what can you do about it?'

'First of all, I can expose the truth about what happened inside Bow Street, then, hopefully as the result of the scandal that blows up from that, I'll get authorisation to begin a systematic investigation into those other stations in which similar things are alleged to have happened.'

'But conducting investigations isn't part of your job anymore, is it?'

'That's where you're wrong,' Jack told her. 'I'm authorised to conduct disciplinary enquiries against Met officers who cross the line in the wrong direction, and obviously sexual assaults on prisoners falls into that category.'

'You'll be very unpopular.'

'I don't regard it as part of my duties to be popular. And I have to think of the interests of those poor women hidden away in police cells, at the mercy of constables with wicked intentions.'

'That's the sort of noble sentiment that made me fall in love with you, Jack Enright,' Esther murmured as she snuggled into his shoulder. 'The cottage pie that Polly made for supper is probably dry enough to use as blotting paper by now, so why don't I make you one of your favourite mushroom omelettes? Another whisky to keep you company while I'm gone?'

Percy Enright had assumed many guises in the past, but being a hurdy-gurdy man was a first for him. Nevertheless, it was the best he could come up with, and the old man who regularly played it outside Percy's favourite watering hole in Lamb Street, Hackney, had been more than happy to lend it to Percy in return for what amounted to several months' income from passersby, and had even shown Percy how to hang it around his neck and turn the handle.

The weather had held good for the entire three weeks in which he'd stood across Regent's Park Road, Finchley, turning the handle and collecting donations, while declining several invitations, and financial inducements, from the butcher in front of whose window he'd pitched himself, to 'sling yer 'ook.'

The object of Percy's attention was the row of shops across the road, one of which — the haberdasher's — was numbered 237, the home address of one Charlotte Springer. Presumably she lived in the large residence that sat above the shop, and appeared to spread across the other four shops in the row. It was not unusual for wealthy retail operators to buy up an entire block of shops, operating out of one and renting out the others, in order to take advantage of the residential accommodation above them.

Today was Thursday, and if events transpired as they had on previous Thursdays, then Percy could abandon his temporary career as a street busker and get back to his garden. On each of the previous Thursdays, smartly dressed women had entered the haberdashery and not re-emerged for several hours. The shop, in keeping with its neighbours, boasted large display windows, and Percy could clearly see that it had remained all but empty, the clear implication being that the ladies in question had been ushered upstairs by way of a rear, or internal, access staircase.

True to habit, they began entering the shop at around ten in the morning, and by the middle of the day Percy had counted well over a dozen, no doubt all drinking tea courtesy of Mrs Springer, and discussing their latest plans to come to the aid of their Suffragette colleagues during their next encounter with the guardians of law and order. It was time to walk down the road and hail a cab for the mercifully short journey south to Tufnell Park Road to report his discovery. Since it was halfway home to Hackney anyway, he might even manage a few hours of tending to his runner bean shoots afterwards.

'Found a new career, have we?' Melville asked laconically in response to the sight of the hurdy-gurdy under Percy's arm as he gained admission to his office.

'It has to be better than working for you lot,' Percy muttered as he placed a crumpled piece of paper down on the desk. 'Those are my expenses so far, and before you ask what I've done to earn them, I invite you to send a team of your tame animals to Number Two Hundred and Thirty-seven Regent's Park, Finchley, next Thursday, sometime after ten in the morning. Above the haberdasher's shop at that address you'll find the home of one Charlotte Springer, and if you time it correctly you'll be able to apprehend a considerable number of her Amazons. My account will be sent to you by mail.'

He walked back out to the coach whose driver had been told to wait for him, and he was home in time for a late lunch before he sought the sanctuary of his vegetable patch, and complimented himself on having completed yet another successful mission — hopefully his last.

He was still deluding himself in that manner later that afternoon, when Beattie appeared at the scullery door and shouted that Jack wished to speak to him urgently on the phone.

## CHAPTER TEN

'I'm beginning to associate the taste of Tang Li's meat pie with a nostalgic longing for my garden,' Percy complained to Jack, seated across the table from him shortly after noon the following day. They were seated at their favourite table in Tang Li's Chophouse on the Embankment, only yards from Cleopatra's Needle. 'It's only a matter of time before my runner beans petition for divorce on the grounds of desertion.'

'I can't say the same for the taste of chicken chow mien,' Jack said with a smile, 'but I think you'll find that this case is right up your street.'

'You mean it's in Hackney?' Percy joked.

'No, but it's got "Percy Enright" written all over it. A grubby murder designed to thwart the criminal justice process, and cover up a growing scandal at the very heart of public life. And it's close enough to here for you to pop in for lunch every day that you're investigating it.'

'So go on — ruin my lunch,' Percy invited him.

'It's about this matron system that's been introduced in some police stations in order to protect female and other vulnerable prisoners from being abused.'

'What about it? I only know that it exists, so if you have more information to disclose, give me the details.'

'I only know the bare outline myself, but it seems that these matrons are all women, as you'd expect, and there's no difficulty with that. In fact, if properly administered, the system has the potential to considerably improve both the efficient performance and the reputation of the Met. As you may know,

I've been suggesting for years that we should consider appointing female constables.'

'No doubt under Esther's influence,' Percy put in, 'and I concede that her services have proved invaluable several times in the past. But that was always undercover, and never in uniform.'

Jack waved away the interruption, then continued, 'You have, of course, become aware of the recent public disturbances created by those women calling themselves Suffragettes, thanks to your old friend Melville, and the need to employ Lucy — another woman, let it be noted — undercover in order to identify the ones learning unarmed combat.'

'That's all completed, and I had hoped to spend more time in my garden until you invited me to lunch.'

'Well, obviously, from the way these strident women carry on, they seem determined to get themselves arrested. Two of them succeeded recently, when they started lobbing rocks at a Government building in Whitehall. The incident was witnessed by Lily and Annabelle, you may recall, to the considerable chagrin of Aunt Beattie. Those two women — Ada Wright and Sarah Carwin — got themselves locked up for the night in Bow Street, where they employ those matrons to whom I referred. Despite the existence of those matrons, they were each isolated in empty cells and sexually assaulted by two police constables.'

'I read that allegation in the *Daily Mail*,' Percy told him, 'but I thought it was another exaggeration by a journalist seeking a meaningful career.'

'No, it's true, as I discovered for myself when I was sent by Barrymore to Bow Street in order to investigate. He no doubt hoped that I would be able to report that the allegation was false. But I reported the complete opposite, and Barrymore's not very happy.'

'I can well imagine,' Percy said wryly.

'I learned the truth from a woman who was on duty that evening as a matron, and who was ordered by the station desk sergeant to turn a blind eye to what happened. The cell records were forged in order to cover up the entire business, and they almost got away with it because the station inspector's one of those time-servers eking out his days until pension time. I wanted to launch further investigations into other stations, but the woman who obligingly gave me the information I was intending to use in order to bring down the entire house of cards was murdered last night. Her name was Ethel Merriman, and her body was found in the early hours of this morning, on the riverbank under Waterloo Bridge, on the north side. That's just down the road from Bow Street Police Station, as you'll be well aware. She'd apparently been strangled.'

Percy sighed. 'I take it that you half expected this, hence why you were no doubt eagerly perusing the overnight reports instead of doing what you're paid to do?'

'Correct. I had a feeling that my visit to Bow Street would stir something up, and I *did* warn Ethel not to repeat our conversation to anyone. All the same, I had a bad feeling that she'd be targeted, so I asked my sergeant to run his eyes over the daily crime bulletin sheets and report to me if any of them contained references to Bow Street. It seems that someone compiling the bulletin knew of her former matron status there, and that's how it got picked up.'

'Presumably the local bobbies have been all over it already, so what do you expect from me?' Percy asked.

'A total lack of bias, and no motivation for a further cover-up,' Jack replied. 'The local police investigating Ethel's death will be the colleagues of the very people I suspect of doing her in before she could blow the whistle on the entire corrupt mess. I need your eyes, your ears, your immunity from bribery or threat, and your bloodhound nose.'

'And I need my pudding,' Percy insisted, 'so I hope you brought me a copy of the case file for me to read while I add another inch to my waistline.'

'I move that the Bill be read a second time,' Home Secretary Gladstone boomed across the crowded Commons chamber.

From the Ladies' Gallery above him came the response, 'And I move for votes for women!'

He looked up, and staring down at him was a determined-looking lady whose battle cry was immediately echoed by several others, all demanding, 'Votes for Women!' from where they were ranged behind the railings. Others appeared behind her in order to shower leaflets down on the members below, which when examined were found to contain propaganda from the WSPU. Two of her colleagues began unfurling a wide banner emblazoned with the demand *Votes for Women*; they lowered it towards the upturned faces of the astonished Members seated in their customary benches.

'Seize those interlopers and remove them!' demanded Prime Minister Asquith, and the sergeant at arms, along with several of his staff, raced up to the Ladies' Gallery, only to discover that the original lady — later identified as a Miss Helen Fox — had produced a padlock and chain, and had secured herself to the railings that protected those in the gallery from falling from it. A massive struggle then ensued, as burly attendants first attempted to remove the very thick chain from the grille, then set about trying to remove the grille itself, while Helen Fox succeeded in haranguing the assembly with part of her prepared speech, despite the efforts of the sergeant at arms to stifle her mouth with his gloved hand.

'Mr Speaker,' she bellowed, 'we have listened for too long to the illogical utterances of men who know not what they say. Attend to the women! We demand of this government calling itself Liberal, but which is really the most illiberal…' That was as far as she got before a gloved hand was forced between her teeth.

But she was not the only one in fine voice. Alongside her was another Suffragette, Muriel Mathers, who, while fending off attempts to remove her from the railing by jabbing a member of the sergeant at arms's staff with a hatpin, took up the battle cry: 'For forty years we have listened behind this grille. We, the women of England; we, your wives, sisters and sweethearts…' Whatever she intended to say next was drowned by the noise of the railings finally being heaved out of their sockets, and everyone collapsing in a tangled heap of bodies to the floor of the upper gallery, where the long, trailing skirts of Suffragettes mingled with the uniforms of the sergeant at arms's staff.

The situation was no less chaotic outside in Parliament Square, where hundreds of Suffragettes had gathered in order to celebrate the success of their bolder colleagues in gaining access to the Ladies' Gallery by the simple expedient of applying individually for spectator passes. Uniformed police had been called in once it became apparent that a larger number of women than usual were ranged under and around the statue of the former Richard I, and that they were not simple day-trippers and sightseers. Pitched battles were being waged in several different parts of the square, eventually resulting in fifteen arrests. Many beaten, bedraggled women lay where they'd fallen, ignored by uniformed officers who were only interested in arresting those who were still in a state to be thrown into a paddy wagon and hauled up the road to Westminster Police Station.

Lily had followed hard on the heels of Sarah Millichip when they'd raced round into Parliament Square in response to all the noise, having been incorrect in their belief that the need for their services would be on Cromwell Green. Lily was uncertain about where to start until Sarah shouted, 'Ignore the ones who're making the most noise. They're still conscious, and we need to deal with the head injuries first!'

There was a woman lying at the foot of the statue with blood dribbling from her ear. Sarah leaned down and placed her ear near the woman's lips, then searched in her medicine bag. To Lily's astonishment, she took out a small hand mirror, which she placed an inch from the woman's mouth, then examined closely.

'I thought so,' she muttered. 'This one's dead, I'm afraid. Let's move on to the living.'

'How can you be sure she's dead?' Lily asked.

'She failed the mirror test. It wasn't misted over after I placed it front of her mouth, so there's no breath coming out. Also, the blood coming from her ear was a sure sign of a fractured skull. She was probably thrown into the plinth at the base of the statue, and banged her head on it. Come over here — there's a woman who looks as if she might still be saveable.'

They moved across to another woman, more elderly than most, whose bodice was open where it had presumably been ripped in a struggle with a constable. The smelling salts that Sarah employed did the trick. Then Sarah helped her to her feet, placed two fingers in front of her face and asked her to count them. The woman answered correctly.

'Go home, but use the omnibus,' Sarah ordered her. 'You're probably not suffering from any brain injury, but don't try to walk any great distance, and button up your bodice, unless you want to be identified as an escaping Suffragette.'

Forty minutes later they'd completed their round of the comatose, and it was time to deal with those who were still conscious and crying out in pain from their injuries. 'We'll start with the ones on the ground,' Sarah said, 'since they may have leg injuries.'

The third woman they came to was sobbing quietly and trying to stand, then screaming in pain and falling back down again. Sarah ordered her to lie still, then felt under the woman's long skirts with a practised hand, evoking another scream and a plea to desist. Sarah looked carefully around, then rose to her feet and rescued what looked like an abandoned and splintered police billy club. Then she said, 'Say goodbye to your umbrella, Lily, but all in a good cause.'

Under Sarah's strict instruction, Lily held the billy club and her umbrella on either side of the woman's injured leg while Sarah produced a long length of bandage from her heavy bag, tore it in two, then tied the two pieces firmly across the two side supports that Lily was holding in place. 'You just placed your first broken leg into a splint,' she told Lily, 'but we'll need to call for a wagon or coach to get this lady home. Could you see if there are any cabs in the vicinity, please?'

Lily succeeded in securing the services of a cabbie, who walked into the square and helped Sarah carry the victim to his cab. She then caught sight of a confused-looking Annabelle in the doorway of the Parliament building. She called out loudly, and Annabelle gave her a wave and came walking swiftly over.

'There you are!' Annabelle said in a relieved tone. 'I feared that you might have got yourself arrested.'

'No, I was helping Sarah with the injured,' Lily replied. 'And I saw quite a lot of women running out of where you just came from, straight into the arms of bobbies who arrested them, so you're lucky *you* weren't arrested.'

'I left the gallery when the front rails were ripped out,' Annabelle explained, 'along with a lot of other women. We were stopped at the bottom of the stairs, but I told the two uniformed types who grabbed me that I was a reporter for the *Illustrated London News*, and that my father was a police inspector. They let me go, but not until after one of them had felt up my bosoms, the dirty wretch!'

'That's awful, Annabelle,' Lily sympathised, 'and you should see what these women out here suffered. No wonder they're trying to get their voices heard where it matters, if that's how men get away with treating them.'

'Well, the next one to try that with me will get a hat pin where it hurts,' Annabelle said firmly. 'But I've got an *amazing* story to write, so let's get back to the library.'

'It's almost time to meet Father back at Euston,' Lily reminded her as she looked up at Big Ben, 'and I've still got a few more injured women to help Sarah with, so go and take a seat by that statue thing and wait for me.'

Back inside the House, order of a sort had been restored, but the Speaker had ordered a thirty-minute adjournment before the debate was to resume. Prime Minister Asquith sidled up to Home Secretary Gladstone and lowered his voice to speak in his ear.

'That was an utter disgrace, Bertie, and these women need to be taught a lesson. Commence the force-feeding immediately.'

*

Percy crunched his way down the shingle under Waterloo Bridge and made a mental note that the tide was beginning to ebb as the Thames resumed its inexorable march towards the open sea. He began searching for traces of where the body of Ethel Merriman might have been found, and after a few paces he came across a collection of discarded cigar and cigarette butts. Then he joined up the dots in his mind.

It hadn't rained overnight, and the discarded butts, which had almost certainly come from police officers as they'd examined the body of Ethel Merriman, were dry, and had therefore been safely above the high water mark on the full tide. Ethel's body was reported, in the copy of the police file in Percy's possession, to have also been dry, so it had clearly not been in the Thames at any stage.

This meant that it hadn't been thrown into the river off Waterloo Bridge, which would have been noisy and likely to attract attention in the early morning, when some workers were already making their way to their places of employment. It also told Percy that she hadn't been thrown into the water further downstream on what would have been the incoming tide. The body had been reported by a family of scavengers who regularly worked by night whenever the tide was right, and they could search hopefully for flotsam and jetsam floating up from the docks area downstream.

There was an indented area in the dry gravel a few feet from the discarded butts, where stones of varying sizes had been disturbed. This was almost certainly where Ethel Merriman had been dumped. The remaining question was whether she'd been strangled elsewhere, and her body brought down on a cart then heaved over the low wall that gave access to the beach, or whether she'd been lured to the beach and done to death there.

It made a considerable difference as to where he should continue investigating.

Percy was still ruminating over his options, and studying his copy of the incident report, when he became aware of a shabby individual standing a few feet behind him, watching him furtively. He smiled encouragingly, and the man asked, 'Yer from the police?'

'Do I look like a police officer?' Percy asked with the appropriate degree of displeasure in his face.

The man nodded. 'Yeah, yer does, but if yer sez yer not, then what yer doin' down 'ere, where that woman were done in?'

'How did you know that?' Percy asked. When the man fell silent and looked apprehensive, Percy came up with one of his instant false identities. 'I'm actually from the newspapers, hoping to get more detail than the miserable bobbies up in Bow Street were prepared to disclose about what happened here last night.'

'Is there money in it if I tells yer sumfin' useful?' the man asked.

'That depends what it is, and how useful it proves to be,' Percy replied as he took out his wallet, extracted a pound note and allowed the breeze off the river to flutter it temptingly in his hand.

'I saw what 'appened,' the man replied. 'Me name's 'Arry Birkenshaw, an' I lives up the road there, in a doss 'ouse on Cecil Street. I likes a few drinks, an' the lodgin's superintendent takes it bad if I goes back in wiv a skinful, so I were out 'ere, walkin' it off. It musta bin pretty late, 'cos the Wellin'ton don't chuck out 'til after midnight. Anyroad, I were walkin' along the Embankment over the wall there when I 'ears this 'ere argument, and looked back ter see two blokes givin' grief ter this old tottie.'

'Where *exactly* was this?' Percy asked.

The man indicated the point on the low wall that Percy had climbed over earlier in order to gain access to the beach.

'Just over there. I were further down the Embankment than that, an' I didn't wanna be seen, so I ducked down an' played dead behind the wall.'

'Then what?' Percy prompted him.

'Then one of the blokes — the one I din't want ter see me — grabbed this old trout be the throat an' pushed 'er over the wall onto the beach. Then 'im an' 'is mate dived in after 'er, an' I could see that they was all rollin' around. I thought they was — you know, doin' the business without payin' — then I 'eard Ben shout out, "She's done fer, Mickey, so let's leg it." Then they scarpered off up Savoy Street, an' I took a quick butcher's over the wall, an' she were lyin' there, where the bobbies took 'er away from this mornin', when I were on me way ter work.'

'That's very helpful, Harry,' Percy said as he relinquished the pound note into the man's eager grasp, 'and there's another one of those for you if you can clarify something you just mentioned. You recognised one of the men with the woman, didn't you, only you didn't want him to see you. Why was that?'

Birkenshaw spat on the ground, then replied, 'It were Ben Fuller, weren't it? 'Im what runs me in fer drunk an' incapable every chance 'e gets, rotten bastard. Yer'd never fink as 'ow me an' 'im was at school together, would yer? Lousy pig.'

'You mean that he's a police officer?' Percy asked as he held his breath while extracting the second pound note.

Birkenshaw nodded. 'Yeah, honest ter God 'e 'is. Works out o' that there Bow Street nick, innit? Mind yer, 'e weren't wearin' 'is uniform last night.'

'Thank you yet again, Mr Birkenshaw,' Percy said. 'You've been of more help than you know.'

'Will me name be in the paper?' Birkenshaw asked.

Percy shook his head. 'You wouldn't want Constable Fuller to know who peached on him, would you? But rest assured that he's not likely to be running you in for drunk and incapable ever again.'

# CHAPTER ELEVEN

Evaline Burkitt had refused all food and liquids since her admission to prison several days previously, having been sentenced for throwing a stone at the Prime Minister's railway carriage. Like all her sisters in the WSPU she'd claimed political status, and when it was refused she'd followed the lead of those before her and gone on hunger strike. She was now about to become a victim of the cruel new policy implemented by Home Secretary Gladstone.

This time there wasn't just the one female turnkey entering with a food tray, which Evaline refused without even looking at what she was being offered. There were six of them this time, and after the first of them had taken the tray back into the corridor and laid it down on the floor, they all moved in on her and held her down on the hard slab that passed for a bed. She was pinned down by her ankles, knees and shoulders, and while she was wriggling a man entered, wearing a white overall and carrying a tube and a container.

Evaline's head was gripped firmly from behind, and a sheet was tied under her chin. Half anticipating what was to follow, she tried her best to free her head, and set her teeth in a vice-like clench, defying anyone to open it as she took short, harsh breaths through her nose. Her eyes closed involuntarily as she fought against the sensation of what must, to judge by the strength of it, be a man's attempts to force open her mouth using a steel bar of some sort. It was pressed against her gums until the pain became so unbearable that she involuntarily unclenched her teeth. Then came the agony of a screw mechanism cranking her lips apart until there was a gap large enough to force a rubber tube down her throat that resulted in a gagging sensation.

After what seemed like an eternity, she heard a man advising her assailants, 'That'll do, ladies.' Then there was the burning sensation of the tube being pulled roughly out again.

She rolled over and vomited all over the floor, and when she was able to open her eyes again her cell was empty.

'The man you want is called Ben Fuller,' Percy told Jack over the telephone once he got home to Hackney. 'He's a uniformed constable attached to Bow Street, and I have a witness who saw him, along with another man, attack Ethel Merriman and leave her for dead — as she almost certainly was — on the shingle under Waterloo Bridge.'

'And what do you suggest that I do with this information?' Jack asked.

'Not my problem,' Percy replied. 'You asked me to find out who killed your only witness to what went on inside Bow Street on the evening that those two women were in there, and I have. You now have the straightforward part.'

'What's so straightforward about interrogating a murder suspect when I don't have any current operational authority?'

'You have the authority to conduct disciplinary enquiries, don't you? And I can't imagine an action more likely to bring discredit upon the Met than one of its officers silencing a vital witness to a gross miscarriage of procedural rules, leading to the violation of prisoners. Use your imagination, Jack.'

'It's hardly an easy task, even so,' Jack complained, and he heard a distinct snort from Percy on the other end of the line.

'If you want a real challenge, come up here and join me for supper — Beatrice's threatening to inflict one of her casseroles on me. Good luck with the interview.'

*

'This is potentially explosive!' Emmeline told Annabelle as they walked under the remaining foliage of the plane trees in Bedford Square, the leaves they had already shed forming a crunchy carpet under their boots. 'We'll have a pot of tea in a minute, then I'll pass on these dreadful accounts of force-feeding that some of our members have succeeded in smuggling out of Holloway, courtesy of the Reverend Shanklin. When you bring your unique talents to bear on what I give you, the world will have to sit up and take notice. The *Daily Mail* have already asked for what they call "urgent copy" from the mysterious Anthony Pickford.'

'I just hope I can do it justice,' Annabelle replied hesitantly. 'It's *so* awful that I can hardly bring myself to believe it. Aren't those wicked prison people breaking the law with what they're doing?'

'That remains to be seen, dear. Hopefully your writing will prod the public into demanding answers from those who control these things.'

In the event, Annabelle's words stunned the reading public, caused a furore in Parliamentary circles, and not only provoked intense debate among medical professionals but led to a legal challenge.

She'd been supplied with almost a dozen accounts of the realities of force-feeding from those who'd suffered it inside Holloway, all of them dictated first-hand to a sympathetic clergyman who'd successfully argued his right to visit those imprisoned within his parish. Annabelle had then converted them into three separate stories, and Emmeline had kept the best of them, sent the second-best to *The Clarion*, and the third one to an eager editor on the staff of the *Daily Mail.* It had been the last of these that had become typeset dynamite on the breakfast tables of the literate, and had led to heated discussions on omnibuses, inside railway carriages, and in the smoking rooms of reputable gentlemen's clubs up and down the nation. Then the medical experts waded in by way of articles and learned opinion papers in their professional journals.

As might have been expected, the most vociferous professional opinions against the morality, and even the medical wisdom, of force-feeding came from those sympathetic to the Suffragette cause. Chief among these was the respected medical commentator Charles Mansell-Moullin, whose wife Edith was a prominent promoter of women's causes. It was his opinion, voiced in the *British Medical Journal*, that this was not, as some argued, 'hospital treatment' akin to that administered to the criminally insane or those too weak to feed themselves, but was, if administered as it was alleged to be against imprisoned Suffragettes, 'a foul libel. Violence and brutality have no place in hospital.'

He received support, this time in *The Observer* newspaper, from eminent surgeon Forbes Ross, who described force-feeding as 'an act of brutality beyond common endurance.' It might well have been the practice in mental asylums as a last resort, he conceded, but it was almost always fatal.

Inevitably there were contrary opinions, and chief among these came from Dr Frederick Mott, a Government pathologist, who claimed never to have encountered fatalities in over ten years of force-feeding in mental asylums. Dr William Cassels, a pioneer of force-feeding in Winson Green Prison in Birmingham, justified the force used in such procedures on the spurious grounds that 'recalcitrant, hostile and uncooperative' prisoners made it necessary by their resistance.

The use of force necessitated by the refusal of prisoners to eat raised serious ethical issues for the profession. On the one hand, it was argued that the Hippocratic Oath that they swore at the beginning of their professional lives required that they intervene to preserve a life that would otherwise end due to starvation, citing the use of nasal or gastric intervention when the patient was incapable of self-feeding. Against this was the counter-argument that consent was essential prior to any invasion of the patient's body whenever the patient was in a condition to give it, and that to proceed without such consent was at the very least criminal assault, and in extreme circumstances a form of torture.

Annabelle had readily adopted the words of one of those whose experiences had been obtained by the Reverend Shanklin, in a letter smuggled out of Strangeways Prison in Manchester, where Hannah Sheppard had been subjected to force-feeding despite already suffering from a stomach ulcer. While not revealing her sources, Annabelle wrote: *This brave woman assures us that what she endured was, in her words, "torture of those on whom it is inflicted. As such, it is repugnant to all modern ideas of punishment, and is a return to the dark ages of barbarism." There can be few right-minded Christians who could deny this.*

It was not long before those opposed to Asquith's Liberal Government sought to make political capital out of what had been rattling around the popular press for several weeks. During one particular Question Time in the House, Keir Hardie, the founder of the Labour Party and its Parliamentary leader, challenged Gladstone to deny that such 'an act of brutality beyond human endurance' was almost guaranteed to result in the death of those on whom it was inflicted. Gladstone's bland response was that he'd read what Dr Forbes Ross had written in the press, but that the force-feeding being adopted in the case of hunger-striking Suffragettes was of a different nature.

When confronted with the riposte that to Hardie's knowledge Gladstone had recently received a memorial signed by well over a hundred doctors, whose collective opinion was that the practice was 'unwise and inhuman', the Home Secretary replied that he had referred the memorial to the then current Physician Royal, Sir Richard Douglas Powell. He had been assured by him that while 'it would be an exaggeration to say that the method of artificial feeding is wholly free from the possibilities of accident with those who forcibly resist', no such cases had come to his knowledge, and 'it may be remarked that patients have been so fed successfully for years.'

The following day, again during Question Time, the topic broadened into the wider issue of granting political status to Suffragette prisoners, which had led to the force-feeding measures in the first place. Gladstone no doubt felt himself to be on firmer ground as he replied, 'No legal definition of "political prisoner" has ever been attempted, and if it means that persons in quest of a political object who break windows, throw missiles into political meetings or crowded streets, and are guilty of disorderly and violent conduct are to be free from the ordinary consequences of the law, my answer is a distinct negative. The public has to be considered. Further, public officials have the same right to protection as private persons, though they may be policemen, prison officials, or even Cabinet ministers.'

That seemed to beg an important question that was far from settled in many minds.

'What am I s'posed ter 'ave done wrong?' Ben Fuller asked truculently as he sought to brazen out the disciplinary meeting to which he'd been summoned by Jack, who was equally determined not to reveal his own uneasiness at using this process as a covert suspect interview designed to expose a murderer.

'I'd probably put that question to Ethel Merriman, if I had the opportunity,' he replied as he stared remorselessly into Fuller's eyes. 'And I have a witness who can testify as to why that won't be possible.'

'D'yer know where's she's gone?' Fuller asked blandly. 'She ain't bin seen around Bow Street fer a day or two, an' 'er old man's a bit concerned.'

Jack smiled. 'You must be the only person attached to Bow Street who hasn't heard what happened to her, Fuller. Her body was lobbed into the Thames after she was murdered, and it would have taken two people. My witness says that you were one of them.'

'Then yer witness is either lyin' or in need of a new pair of eyes,' Fuller said, smirking. 'If she were lobbed inter the river, 'ow come 'er body were still dry when they found it?'

'So you *do* know what happened to her,' Jack replied in triumph. 'It would still have taken two people to get her over that wall.'

'But only one ter strangle 'er,' Fuller pointed out.

Jack's smile widened. 'Did I say she was strangled? I don't remember saying that.'

'Well, that's the word around Bow Street,' Fuller replied sourly, clearly infuriated at having given away more than he intended.

It was now an appropriate time for Jack to offer the man a way out. 'If she *was* strangled, by whoever,' he said, 'then it could have been an accident, when two men were endeavouring to persuade her to keep quiet about something.

And if I knew what that something was, I might find it easier to accept that it *was* an accident, brought about by an eagerness to shut her up.'

'It were Tommy Atkinson,' Fuller muttered.

'What was it that this Tommy Atkinson did, exactly?' Jack asked as casually as he could.

'Strangled the stupid cow. She kept on insistin' that she'd said nowt ter the nosey copper what come from the Yard ter stick 'is oar inter sumfin what were none of 'is business in the fust place.'

'*I* was that nosey copper, Fuller. It was made my business by Chief Superintendent Barrymore, who wanted to know if it was true that normal procedures were ignored on an evening when two Suffragette women were occupying cells on the ground floor corridor inside Bow Street nick. They claim to have been, shall we say, *interfered with*. You could tell me more about it in return for my more ready acceptance that what happened to Ethel Merriman was indeed an accident.'

'Yer mean that it'll be written off as an accident, an' that it were Tommy Atkinson what squeezed too 'ard?' Fuller asked eagerly.

Jack nodded. 'That's certainly one way of looking at the facts, but only when I've learned more about what happened to the Suffragettes.'

'Well, they made it all too easy, din't they?' Fuller said. 'Allowin' us ter put our own women inter the nick — and 'ave 'em paid fer doin' it. Then pretendin' as 'ow the tastier women what we arrest is in no danger of bein' felt up, an' maybe a bit more'n that. Like them two Suffragist types.'

'Suffragettes,' Jack corrected him.

'Yeah, well, whatever yer calls 'em, they was right tasty, so Ethel were told ter look the other way while they was put inter a cell each, then Tommy an' Bert Tranter went in an' give 'em what for.'

'The "Tommy" to whom you referred was the same Tommy Atkinson who went on to strangle Ethel when it was believed that she'd peached on him?'

'Yeah — 'e were that scared 'e were gonna lose 'is job.'

'And the other man who went into the cells where Ada Wright and Sarah Carwin had been isolated — his name was Herbert Tranter?'

'Yeah — will 'e get ter know as 'ow I peached on 'im? Only 'e's a big bloke.'

'That remains to be seen,' Jack replied, 'but do you know of any other police stations in which such things take place?'

'Yer could try Westminster, or Gray's Inn Road, or maybe Cannon Street. That's where them Suffragists get taken to after they's bin arrested, an' them's the ones that the men prefers. A better class of personal 'ygiene, and nice bodies, since they's rich and well fed.'

'Yes, thank you, I get the general picture,' Jack replied as he suppressed the urge to strangle the life out of Fuller. 'You can go now, and while you may not be facing a murder charge, it might be a good idea to start looking for another way of earning your living.'

Jack's elation was short-lived when, the following morning, he sought a meeting with Barrymore and recounted the outcome of his meeting with Fuller, and his proposal for what should be done next.

'Do you mean to say that you're seriously proposing to drop a murder charge against one of those who strangled to death a woman employed by the Met, simply in order to unearth an alleged flaw in one of our systems?' Barrymore asked angrily.

'And what business did you have conducting a murder investigation in the first place? While you're about it, explain how you came to be in possession of a case file from Bow Street. Have you disobeyed that instruction I gave you some time ago, when you were sticking your nose into a murder enquiry in Holborn in which your sister was a major suspect?'

'No, sir,' Jack explained as patiently as he was able. 'It began purely as a disciplinary enquiry, when I learned from an independent witness that Fuller had been seen arguing with a woman I'd interviewed inside Bow Street the previous day — on your direct instruction, if you recall.'

'But by then you knew that the woman in question had been murdered, did you not? Incidentally, how did you acquire *that* knowledge?'

'Her murder was reported in the normal way, in the overnight incident bulletin that I peruse daily.'

'Which you have no obvious business "perusing", as you put it, but leave that aside. You knew that she'd been murdered, but you're asking me to believe that when you interviewed this man Fuller as someone seen arguing with her on the night she was murdered, it never even occurred to you that he might have been the one who killed her?'

'With respect, sir, we're in danger of missing a vitally important point. This man Fuller disclosed to me that the system we have in place to protect vulnerable women taken into custody isn't working. The women who're being selected as matrons are vulnerable to pressure from officers attached to the station in which they're based, who in many cases are their husbands or friends, to look the other way while gross abuse is inflicted.'

'Not in every case, surely?' Barrymore reasoned.

Jack let out a frustrated sigh. 'We won't know unless we investigate further, will we? I've been told of at least three other stations where such abuse may happen.'

'And you're seeking my approval to go charging in there with allegations that female prisoners, and most obviously Suffragettes, are being systematically subjected to sexual assaults while those appointed to prevent it just stand aside and let it happen?'

'Yes, sir. We owe a duty of care to these women, and for that matter, *all* vulnerable prisoners, to ensure that appropriate procedures are in place to protect them. We need to eradicate any possibility that the system we currently have in place has been corrupted.'

'Are you completely mad, Enright?' Barrymore shouted. 'Can you imagine what the newspapers will make of that, during this sensitive time when questions are being raised in the House concerning alleged institutional brutality against Suffragettes in custody?'

'I thought we might perhaps be more concerned with ensuring that we have an efficient system in place to *prevent* that,' Jack replied hotly, 'when clearly, at present, we do not.'

'You're to take this matter no further, Enright, do you understand?' Barrymore shouted even louder. 'Not even to the extent of charging this man Fuller with murder, because of the risk that it will lead indirectly to news leaking out as to why this matron was killed. Have I made myself plain, or do you want it in writing?'

'But, sir!' Jack began to protest, then stopped when he saw the colour of Barrymore's face.

'End of interview,' Barrymore announced as he picked up his pen and made an obvious gesture of perusing some papers on his desk. 'Go back downstairs and do what you're appointed to do, and let's hear no more of this nonsense.'

The political sensitivity of the situation to which Barrymore had alluded was highlighted even more strongly a few weeks later, in early December, when one of the Suffragettes who'd been force-fed chose to raise a legal challenge against what she'd endured.

Mary Leigh had been sentenced to two weeks' imprisonment in Winson Green Prison, Birmingham, for her part in a demonstration at a public meeting addressed by Prime Minister Asquith, and in accordance with standard Suffragette policy she'd immediately gone on hunger strike. The response by the prison authorities was swift and brutal, involving force-feeding though a nasal tube that was painful, humiliating and distressing. Convinced that her basic rights had been violated, she celebrated her release by commencing an immediate legal action for damages, citing Home Secretary Gladstone as the defendant.

*Leigh v Gladstone* was destined to be a watershed precedent concerning the right of individuals to starve themselves to death in a Government institution when the case was put before Mr Justice Avory in the King's Bench Division of the High Court in December of that year. For the plaintiff, Leigh, it was argued that the force-feeding to which she'd been subjected had constituted an unlawful assault, given that it had occurred without her consent, and contrary to her freedom of choice not to eat. The defendant's argument was that the action had been necessary in order to preserve Leigh's life, and that the State had a duty to protect her life while she was in its care.

The verdict was in favour of the authorities, and established the precedent that what lawyers called 'the doctrine of necessity' justified the act of force-feeding, and that the State's duty to preserve a life overrode the fundamental right of autonomy over one's body that every individual possessed, whenever failing to act could result in death or serious harm.

The popular press flew into a frenzy. Articles by commissioned experts jostled for column space with letters from concerned observers, whose content was largely dictated by the social class to which the patrons of those newspapers belonged.

# CHAPTER TWELVE

Percy looked up from where he was pulling Brussels sprouts from the row of plants. It was two weeks before Christmas, and they'd already endured some freezing weather, so in accordance with the old gardening adage that you could pick sprouts once they'd had their first touch of frost he was hoping to bag up enough of them for the traditional Enright family gathering at the Watford house on Boxing Day.

The fixed smile on the face of the man walking down the path towards him made him more closely resemble a mannequin in a gentlemen's outfitter's window than he had on the previous occasion, and Percy growled up at him, 'I don't suppose you come bearing season's greetings from Melville?'

'First, the usual invitation.'

'Get in the coach or else?'

'Precisely. *Then* a Merry Christmas.'

'I think I'd rather be shot dead among my brassicas. At least then there'd be some living thing to note the cause of my passing. Make it quick and merciful, in return for this bucket of sprouts.'

'I was educated at a public school,' the man told him, 'and we learned from experience never to touch them.'

'On this occasion,' Percy insisted, 'I don't intend to get changed out of my gardening clothes, so let's see how "M" takes to having mud all over his Axminster, shall we?'

An hour later, Melville frowned over the top of his desk and made a point of giving Percy's horticultural attire a long, sweeping look. 'There was no need to dress for the occasion,' he said disapprovingly.

'My Santa Claus costume's still at the tailor's. I notice that you had time to erect a Christmas tree in the hallway back there; were the things hanging from it angels, or the souls of long-executed public servants?'

'Your humour is hardly appropriate for the traditional observance of "peace on earth, and goodwill towards all men", which is all to the good, since I want you to hunt me one down and ruin his career. I take it that the fee for your last mission, extortionate though it was, was duly received?'

'Received and spent on prayers for my immortal soul,' Percy replied sourly. 'Given that you want something from me, will we be sitting down to Christmas lunch in an hour or so?'

'Lunch, certainly,' Melville confirmed, 'but not turkey and sprouts. More like cottage pie and green beans. Your speciality, I seem to recall.'

'I've never cultivated cottage pie,' Percy replied with a deadpan expression, 'so what do you want this time?'

'Have you ever heard of a man called Anthony Pickford?'

'Can't say I have, but then I'd hazard a guess that he's never heard of Percy Enright either, so that puts us on a level footing.'

Melville reached out, picked up several copies of the *Daily Mail*, and pushed them in Percy's direction. 'While we anticipate lunch, you might want to take a look at that lot. Muck-raking journalism at its best, verging on the seditious, and I want the man identified, followed, hauled in and silenced. Journalistically speaking, of course. He won't go to gaol until he's convicted, but that should be sufficient to stem the flow of his pernicious drivel.'

Percy gathered up the newspapers and began to look casually through them. They were all fairly recent, and one of them had a front-page article that had been heavily underscored in red pen.

'Don't go automatically for the racing pages,' Melville instructed him, 'but read the alleged "news" items in them that are accredited to this Anthony Pickford. Particularly that last one, in which he *definitely* overstepped the mark.'

'Is this your own editing?' Percy asked.

Melville nodded. 'Pure sedition, if not actual treason. Read that, then you'll appreciate why I want him closed down.'

Percy read the article on the front page of a very recent issue of the *Daily Mail*, and whistled softly as he took in the powerful rhetoric that in effect likened the current British Government to the Tsarist regime in Russia that had been universally condemned for its brutality by every westernised nation, including those within the massive British Empire. It was well known that thirty years previously, a group of political prisoners opposed to the harsh rule of the Romanov dynasty had gone on hunger strike inside their gaol in St Petersburg. The authorities had resorted to force-feeding, and the general who had ordered it had proudly added that he had ordered coffins in advance for the victims. Pickford had written:

*While the Christian world once recoiled in horror at what were described at the time as the 'atrocities' inflicted on political prisoners during the brutal retaliation of the Tsar and his evil executioners, chief of which was the practice of force-feeding that was accepted as invariably fatal, our own so-called 'Liberal' Government sees nothing wrong, a generation later, in inflicting the same slow, lingering and agonising death on those who are not even regarded as political prisoners, whatever justification that may provide for such bestial practices . Why should we condemn the Russian Tsar and his servants of Satan when, in our own country, those who claim to rule us as Christian Liberals are no better than them? Do we have a Government that gives a damn about the sanctity of human life, and if not, then is it not time that we did?*

'That's telling them,' Percy said with a smirk as he looked up from what he'd been reading.

Melville scowled back. 'Don't tell me that you actually agree with all that rubbish? It's openly inviting its readers to bring down the Government, which makes it seditious. Mr Gladstone is most put out, and has left me in no doubt that he wants this man taken to a place where his treasonous ramblings can't be published anymore. Back to South Africa, presumably, where he's apparently from, according to my initial enquiries.'

Percy sighed. 'Surely it's not beyond the resources of MO5, or whatever number it's been allocated *this* week, to identify one man? Why do I smell a huge rat here? Why me?'

'Why do you think?' Melville replied. 'You're our first choice when we wish to hide our hand beneath a glove puppet. How would it look if it were known that the Home Secretary's only response to being compared to a Russian dictator was to eliminate the person who made that comparison?'

'So if I find him, he's dead?' Percy asked with a downturned mouth that reflected his obvious distaste.

Melville shrugged. 'Our — *your* — job is to identify and locate him. I have no instruction beyond that.'

Percy's face creased in disgust. 'My wife insists that I accompany her to church on those Sundays when I've run out of excuses. One of the few benefits I derive from that is a vague familiarity with the Scriptures. What you just said reminds me of the words of Pontius Pilate when he condemned Christ to the cross, and rejected the opportunity to release him when the local population chose Barabbas instead.

His precise words were, "I am innocent of this man's blood." I hope you can look at yourself in the mirror if I find this bloke Pickford, and he's never seen again.'

'The good news is that your fee will be twice what we paid you last time,' Melville told him through narrow lips that were white with fury. 'The bad news is that your invitation to lunch just got cancelled.'

'There's probably some truth in the old saying that "It's too cold for snow,"' Percy muttered as he kicked a cloud of hoar frost from the top of the grass on Jack's rear lawn. He'd been banished there by Beattie with his pipe after a splendid Boxing Day lunch, complete with Hackney-reared Brussels sprouts. 'It's on days like this that I almost feel like giving up smoking, given that I'm sent out to the garden to do it, but at least I can warm my hands up on the pipe bowl. When do you think this Arctic weather will ease?'

'I'm hoping it gets worse,' Jack said. 'There's a history of the points freezing up on the Euston line, which with a bit of luck will mean that I can't get into work. It's a waste of effort anyway, during this disrupted time between Christmas and the New Year, when I can't conduct recruitment interviews.'

'I'm using the same excuse with the latest job that Melville's dumped on me,' Percy replied. 'He wants me to track down a journalist called Anthony Pickford, and since the newspaper offices are closed for the holidays I've got a plausible justification for waiting until we're into 1910, and all that the New Year has in store for us.'

'That name rings a bell with me,' Jack mused. 'Didn't he write something about our dear Mr Asquith being no better than the Tsar of Russia?'

'More or less,' Percy confirmed. 'Melville wants him hauled up for "sedition" — or at least, Gladstone does, only they don't want to be *seen* to be persecuting him, so they've asked me to find him and hand him over. Well, when I say "asked", it was more of a demand, for which I'll be paid handsomely. I feel like Judas, to be perfectly honest with you.'

'At least you've been allowed to go after your quarry,' Jack said, sighing. 'I have every justification for raiding most of the nicks where those Suffragettes have been held recently, in order to prove that the matron system isn't working, and indeed is making the problem worse. The very women who're supposed to be protecting Suffragettes while they're in custody are connected in some way to those men who're guilty of the sexual abuse, and are therefore vulnerable to pressure to keep quiet about what goes on.'

'Like that Ethel Whatshername whose murderer I identified for you?'

'Precisely. I got a confession from that man Fuller who you pointed me towards, then Barrymore told me to take the matter no further. He's terrified in case it gets out that the matron system isn't working, and I've got nothing more to go on in order to build a case for the entire system being corrupt. Some formal complaints from Suffragettes who've been subjected to sexual misconduct while in custody, despite the existence of matrons, would be ideal, but I've been rudely ordered to stick to recruitment.'

'So neither of us is looking forward to getting back to work,' Percy observed with a wry smile, 'but at least there should be tea and mince pies awaiting us in the sitting room, along with the extended Enright family.' With that, they made their way back to the house.

'We were wondering when a combination of the cold air and the call of mince pies would lure you back inside,' Beattie commented drily to Percy as they re-entered the sitting room, 'but now that you're back, you can add your no doubt cynical opinion to the ongoing discussion regarding the demand for Asquith to dissolve Parliament and call a General Election over the Suffragette issue.'

'I was under the impression that it's the king who dissolves Parliament,' Percy replied sarcastically as he reached for a mince pie.

'At least wait until Alice's poured you a cup of tea before you add even more to your waistline,' Beattie insisted, briefly smiling at Jack and Esther's maid. 'I would have thought that the disgraceful amount you put away over lunch would have filled even *your* digestive warehouse.'

'Who's calling for Asquith to throw in the towel?' Jack asked.

It was his brother-in-law Teddy who answered, 'It was all over the newspapers just before Christmas. There's a demand from Labour leader Keir Hardie that Asquith's Government resign over its inability to control those Suffragette people.'

'And does Mr Hardie have any suggestion regarding how *he* proposes to deal with them?' Percy asked.

'None that he mentioned,' Teddy conceded.

'He wouldn't want to take them on unarmed, from what I saw of their fighting skills when I did that undercover job for Uncle Percy,' Lucy put in. 'They're being taught some *very* nasty tricks, let me tell you.'

'They'll surely need them if the police carry on treating them the way they have been,' Esther pointed out. 'What Lily and Annabelle described of what they saw that afternoon in Whitehall was truly *awful*, and there can be no justification for grown men behaving like that towards women who are merely trying to make a political point.'

'It's the way they're going about it,' Jack insisted. 'For as long as they continue to break the law, the politicians will be able to argue that they're not fit to have the vote. They're defeating their own objective.'

'A cheap excuse from those not prepared to consider the matter on its merits,' Beattie suddenly chimed in. 'The issues *should* be debated calmly and dispassionately, and it's the very refusal of the politicians to accede to that simple and valid request that's provoked the campaigners down the road of violence. But Esther also has a good point: the police shouldn't be allowed to resort to brute force in order to stifle protests from women who — apart from the warriors Lucy mentioned — aren't equipped by Nature to defend themselves. And by all accounts,' she added as her lips turned down with distaste, 'it doesn't stop when they've been arrested and hauled away. Why else would it be necessary to appoint those matrons to guard their interests once they're locked away in prison cells?'

'For what it's worth, I can tell you in confidence that the matron system's got flaws that no-one in authority will admit to, as Uncle Percy can confirm from his recent enquiry on my behalf,' Jack replied. 'But it's hardly a topic for family discussion around the mince pies at Christmas.'

'But how else can we remain reliably informed?' Teddy persisted. 'There have to be advantages to having someone on the inside who can tell us what's really going on, hidden behind locked doors. Otherwise we have to rely on what we read in the papers, which can't even be trusted to get the weather reports right.'

'Jack was complaining, weeks ago, that there's an inherent problem with the matron system,' Esther told them all. 'It's failing to live up to its promise.'

All eyes turned to Jack, who dropped his gaze to the tea table and muttered, 'You only have yourselves to blame if you end up even more despondent and cynical about police procedures, but Esther's right. If you must know, I've unearthed some evidence to suggest that my worst fears have come true, and that the policy of appointing matrons from among police wives and associates has made it possible to coerce such women to look the other way, while policemen commit terrible acts.'

'So horrible things really *are* happening to women inside police cells, as the newspapers report?' Lucy asked.

'Correct, I'm afraid. And before you ask what I'm doing about it, you should know that my ultimate superior at the Yard has forbidden me from going out and getting the evidence to prove it.'

'That's outrageous!' Teddy gasped.

'It is,' Jack agreed. 'It's only a matter of time before one of them gets killed — not as the result of force-feeding, but because of physical attacks on them by police officers sworn to protect them. As for the matrons themselves, one of them has already been murdered for seeking to reveal the truth.'

'He's not exaggerating,' Percy added. 'I was the one who brought him the evidence of that.'

'So what are *you* doing about it?' Beattie demanded of Percy, who gave a despondent shrug and nodded in Jack's direction.

'As Jack already indicated, it's his problem, and he can do nothing, by official command from the highest level.'

'You're not serious?' Beattie demanded.

'He is. We both are,' Percy replied despondently.

'Let Jack speak,' Beattie admonished him, and Jack spelt out in greater detail how he'd been ordered by Barrymore to make no further enquiry into how badly the system might be letting down vulnerable prisoners.

The dismal silence that followed was broken by Beattie's sharp observation: 'On that dreadful day in Whitehall, when Lily and Annabelle were unwise enough to wander into that disgraceful scene that led to women being dragged away by their hair, it was only due to God's infinite mercy that they weren't mistaken for rioters themselves, and taken into custody. It could have been *they* who were mishandled in the cells! Two innocent fresh-faced girls, who would no doubt present a great temptation to brutish men with wicked intentions. God save us, it doesn't bear thinking about!'

'That's why I'm so frustrated at not being able to do anything to prevent what's happening,' Jack explained. 'Whatever you may think of the political views of these women, or even their methods, just imagine if they were people we knew. Girls or women like Lily, Annabelle, Lucy or Esther. I'm determined to expose the existing system and have it replaced with one that engages women who're not so easily corrupted when it comes to ensuring that nothing terrible happens to those protestors once they're in custody.'

'Well, when you do, let me know!' Beattie burst out, to a ribald chuckle from Percy.

'For once it wasn't *me* who talked a family member into something. Let it be noted that she did it all by herself.'

By mid-January, the earth was so hard with frost that not even a sharp spade could penetrate it. Percy therefore abandoned his beans and set about earning his latest commission. His first port of call were the offices of the *Daily Mail* in Northcliffe

House, where he eventually found himself sitting across the desk from the news editor, Samuel Bentinck. Percy was posing as some official from the Foreign Office, having flashed his crown-crested entry pass to a long-ago horticultural show, which had once again been enough to fool anyone who asked for proof of his identity.

'You wanted to know about Anthony Pickford?' Bentinck asked. 'Might I be allowed to know what interest the Foreign Office might have in him?'

'You may,' Percy oozed, 'and I might add that my presence here today is entirely in the best interests of your newspaper, and its revered proprietor Mr Harmsworth. We have reason to believe that Mr Pickford hails from the former Orange Free State, which as you will be aware recently became part of the new nation of South Africa under legislation passed by our own Parliament. However, regrettably, there still remain some Boer factions left in what used to be their independent republic, and we have reason to believe that Mr Pickford's motivation for being over here is the subversive one of undermining the legislation by casting aspersions on the fitness of the current Liberal Government — hence his recent fulminations against Government policy towards the Suffragette movement.'

'And you believe that this may have compromised the newspaper?'

'It's obviously possible,' Percy wheedled, 'that in all innocence you were the means by which subversive views were conveyed to your vast reading public, which of course could be a source of potential embarrassment to your proprietor, given the extent of his involvement with Mr Asquith's Government, which holds him in such high regard.'

'So you wish me to take no more items from Mr Pickford until you've established his bona fides?'

'That, certainly, but we would also be most appreciative if you could advise us of where he may be currently located, and in what circles he moves, in order that we may conduct our own enquiries regarding those bona fides.'

'I can't really help you there, I'm afraid,' Bentinck replied with what seemed like genuine regret. 'We get all his copy from two separate sources — first of all, *The Clarion*, which is based in Manchester but has a small office here in London, in Gough Square, just off Fleet Street. The second is that broadsheet — one could hardly call it a newspaper — put out by the Women's Social and Political Union, or the "Suffragettes", as everyone now calls them. It's called *Votes for Women*, and it was the editor, a woman called Emmeline Pethick-Lawrence, who first introduced us to the writing of Anthony Pickford. I've never actually met him, but I was told he recently arrived from South Africa and is anxious to establish himself as a journalist here in London. If you find him, please ask him to contact me, and tell him that there's a full-time position for him here at the *Daily Mail*.'

'Which of those two papers do you suggest I go to next?' Percy asked. 'From what you've just told me, that Suffragette rag sounds like the better bet.'

'I agree,' Bentinck replied. 'You'll find them hidden away in an office that they rent from St. Clements Press, a hole-in-the-wall printing concern in Clements Inn Passage, in the city. Good luck, and remember to pass on my invitation to Mr Pickford.'

'You don't impress me with your fancy title,' Emmeline Pethick-Lawrence told Percy an hour later, her jaw jutting in defiance, 'but I assume that you have authority to search these premises?'

'You may so assume,' Percy replied with a confident grin as he made a mental note to ask Melville to give him a retrospective one. 'Now, if you'd be so good?'

'Help yourself, but you won't find Mr Pickford here,' he was assured.

For the next hour, he occupied himself opening every drawer, examining the contents of every cabinet, and looking under every suspicious pile of previous editions of *Votes for Women*, all to no avail. The smug smile on Emmeline's face was beginning to raise his blood pressure, and he finally asked, 'How do you contact this Mr Pickford?'

'He contacts us, whenever he has something worthwhile to write. He then sends in his copy, and it goes to the printers along with everything else.'

'Have you ever met him?'

'Anthony Pickford? No,' Emmeline told him, 'but I'd very much like to. Our sales have increased beyond all expectations since he began writing for us, and his latest offering, regarding the pitiful failure of Mr Asquith and his band of acolytes to prevent the sexual abuse of our members while detained in prison cells, promises to bring down an entire Government. It went to press an hour ago, but you can buy a copy if you wait outside in the street for a few hours.'

Percy was seething as he descended the staircase on his way out, but stopped dead when he heard a rhythmic clonking noise from the other side of a glass-fronted door on the half-landing that he'd reached. The sign on the panel read 'St. Clements Press', and hadn't the man at the *Daily Mail* told him that they printed *Votes for Women*? And hadn't that dreadful woman upstairs told him that her latest scandal sheet was in the process of being printed?

'Nothing ventured, nothing gained,' he reminded himself as he pushed open the door and let his ears adjust to the noise before shouting at the man sitting at a table on which he was inserting type into a tray with the aid of a soft hammer. Percy flashed his false identity card, and the man sighed, stood up, walked to the machine that was clonking out single pages of what might well be the latest issue of *Votes for Women*, turned it off, then turned back to address Percy.

'Whaddya want?' he demanded.

Percy cut to the chase. 'Whatever you can give me on Anthony Pickford.'

'Yer want the original, the typed version, or the one I were busy knocking inter typeface when yer interrupted me?'

'Give me the original,' Percy demanded. If he couldn't meet the elusive Anthony Pickford, at least he could get a sample of his handwriting for comparison purposes, should that ever become relevant.

The man reached inside a drawer of his desk and drew out several sheets of what looked like a schoolchild's exercise book. He slid them across the desk, and Percy looked down at them, then went cold all over.

There would be no need to have *this* particular handwriting compared with anything, since he knew it like the back of his hand. And if he needed comparison material, he had sheets of it at home, from the years in which Annabelle had spent part of her school holidays with Percy and Beattie, writing stories that she'd then read to them by the fire on long, lazy evenings.

It would require all his guile and experience to work his way around *this* setback.

## CHAPTER THIRTEEN

Percy had opted not to go home immediately, but instead was wandering aimlessly through Victoria Park, across the road from his home. He needed to think through the implications of what he'd just learned and decide when — if ever — to reveal it to anyone else. At some stage Jack would need to be advised, if only to prevent him trying to contact Anthony Pickford himself, as part of his ongoing investigations.

Then there was Beattie, who idolised Annabelle, and had done from the first day that she'd met her all those years ago, when Esther had taken her in. The dear, sweet girl with the endearing skill at storytelling would appear to have turned into a campaigner for women's rights, using her gift with words to publish accusations against the current Government that were on the cusp of being seditious. What was he to tell Beattie? Or should he keep silent?

Finally, when, and how, could he confront Annabelle with what he'd learned? And should he? The easy option would be to let her continue, in the hope that her true identity would never be revealed, but that was surely wishful thinking. He was prepared — indeed happy — to lie to Melville, and complain that he'd not succeeded in identifying and locating Pickford, but if he did, would Melville not send others to carry out that task? Didn't he owe it to Annabelle to at least alert her to the fact that if he'd managed to track her down so easily, others would experience little difficulty in doing so?

While he was turning these quandaries over in his head, he found that his feet had taken him, perhaps subconsciously, to the 'pond', as locals called it, despite the London Council proudly declaring it a 'lake'. His memory drifted back to the happy days in which he'd accompanied a starry-eyed, energetic and over-imaginative Annabelle to this very stretch of water, in order that she might sail Jack's old boat and imagine that it was journeying to the Indies, the Americas, or wherever her romantic whim dictated. Then his train of thought was broken as a young boy whizzed past him, gliding across the surface of the water, and Percy realised that the lad was actually skating.

It was not unheard of for the lake in Victoria Park to freeze over in the depths of winter, given that it was relatively shallow even at the centre, and the bitterly cold weather that they'd experienced this past month had at least resulted in one public benefit. He lifted his gaze higher, and counted at least a dozen people, of varying ages, sexes, and skating skills, taking advantage of Nature's gift, and an idea slotted into place like the latch on his garden gate.

He made his way swiftly back across the park, avoiding the paths and taking the direct route across the grass, which crunched in protest under his feet and sent plumes of frost from the toes of his boots. Back home he opted for the scullery door, given the state of his footwear, and he found Beattie in the kitchen, stirring something unknown, and probably inedible, in a large saucepan on the stove.

'I wasn't sure if you'd be home for supper,' she told him, 'so you'll have to take pot luck.'

'I'll also take my life in my hands and ask if what the lucky pot contains is likely to be edible in due course,' he muttered, 'then I'll reveal the brilliant idea I've just had.'

'It's stew,' Beattie replied with a face as frosty as the ground he'd just walked over. 'Given the current weather, we need something nourishing in our stomachs, and earlier today I baked a cinnamon loaf. So you'll be able to sit down to a wholesome meal containing leftover lamb from yesterday, along with some of your stale garden produce. Now, what's this brilliant idea that you claim to have had? It'll be worth hearing, if only for its rarity value.'

'I decided to take a turn in the park on my way home,' Percy continued, undaunted, 'and they're skating on the pond.'

'I hope your brilliant idea wasn't for us to do the same?' she said tersely. 'Much though I'd love to see you skidding across the surface of a frozen pond on your situpon, it wouldn't be very edifying for anyone who knows us.'

'Not us, obviously — Annabelle and Lily.'

'And why would they want to do that?'

'Because it's an opportunity that doesn't come along very often, and they're probably feeling very lethargic, cooped up inside that old house in Watford, unable to go anywhere because of the weather. Well, for once the weather can be made to work to their advantage.'

'Do they own any skates?'

'No idea, but we could always ask. And if they don't, all we'll need is their shoe size and we can get some for them. I'd rather hoped that you'd leap at the chance to have them down here for a day or two, and this would be a perfect excuse to lure them down here.'

'What are you planning?'

'Nothing, why?'

'Well, normally when you think of other people, it's in connection with something that you're plotting, and I don't imagine that this occasion is any different. But if you promise me that you'll be here to share in the hosting duties, I'll give them a call and see if they're interested.'

*

Three days later, Annabelle and Lily had accepted the invitation and arrived with one pair of ice skates between them. Beattie was about to send Percy into town for another pair when Annabelle reassured her, 'It's all right, Aunt Beattie. Lily and I are the same shoe size, and we don't mind sharing, honestly! We can take turns, and I can watch Lily falling over before she does the same for me.'

This arrangement suited Percy admirably. Just before he took the two girls across the road, he crept into the small storage cupboard that he was pleased to call his home office, and extracted the papers he'd acquired from the compositor employed by St. Clements Press. He then hid them in the inside pocket of his heavy outdoor coat, then announced that it was time to brave the freezing fog that hadn't yet lifted from the streets of Hackney.

Annabelle was the first to venture onto the ice, and predictably she was sliding her long trailing skirts along the filmy surface within minutes, as she tried to execute a tight turn, lost her balance, and fell. She grimaced, picked herself up, and made her way to the frosty grass edge of the pond, where she clumped awkwardly up the gentle slope and sat down with a chuckle on the bench from which Percy and Lily had watched her antics. Then she took off the skates and handed them to Lily with the challenge, 'See if you can do any better.'

The time would never be more advantageous, and Percy had rehearsed a thousand times in his head the words that now came to his mouth.

'How is your writing progressing?' he asked disingenuously.

Annabelle smiled. 'It's coming along very well, Uncle Percy, thanks to your encouragement when I was younger. I'm hoping to get something published within the next year or so.'

'In something more uplifting and worthwhile than the *Daily Mail*?' he replied.

Her eyes widened and her smile froze as she said, 'Why would I want to write for that scandal sheet?'

'Because they're happy to publish what you write,' he said calmly as he reached inside his overcoat. 'But I wouldn't advise you to use your real name in future publications, unless you want to be charged with sedition,' he added as he produced the tell-tale sheets like a conjurer with a rabbit.

She blanched visibly, then asked in a small voice, 'Where did you get those?'

'From a very obliging printer,' Percy told her. 'One I managed to track down after learning from a very unfriendly lady named Emmeline Pethick-Lawrence that she'd never met Anthony Pickford. Which is true, in a sense, since she'd only ever met Annabelle Pickering, had she not? What the printer published under your assumed name was eagerly snapped up by the *Daily Mail*, and I read it almost as soon as it was on the streets.'

'What are you going to do about this?' Annabelle asked hoarsely, as she cast an anxious eye across the pond to confirm that Lily was still carving out figures of eight in the centre of it.

'Not what I was commissioned to do,' Percy replied, 'which was to find Anthony Pickford and hand him over for arrest on a charge of sedition. What did you think you were about?'

'I was writing the truth, Uncle Percy,' Annabelle insisted defiantly, 'and if the truth offends you, then I'm sorry. But these women who're seeking nothing more than equality with men in the opportunities that life affords have been treated shabbily, brutally, and illegally, and the very least I can do is give them a voice, using a talent that God has given me.'

'Even though you could end up locked away with them?'

'Particularly then, if it would give me the opportunity to see for myself the wicked things that are inflicted on them once they've been arrested. Not just the force-feeding in prison — that's common knowledge, and freely admitted to by Asquith, Gladstone and their cronies in criminal abuse. What is *not* so well known is what goes on before they even reach the courts. What happens in the police cells, literally behind locked doors, with no-one to come to their assistance.'

'So you alleged in your latest article,' Percy said, nodding. 'But where's your evidence, and what about the women who've been allocated to police stations in order to prevent precisely that sort of thing?'

'You obviously believe the rubbish that's being put out by those with an interest in keeping these matters under wraps, namely the police themselves,' Annabelle retorted. 'Those matron women are either married to the very men who're taking vile advantage of their victims, or threatened to keep their mouths shut. As for my evidence, I have a bundle of statements from the Suffragettes to whom it's happened, who were ignored, both when they were screaming for someone to come to their assistance, and afterwards, when they tried to make formal complaints.'

Percy came instantly alert, then asked, 'Did you know that your Uncle Jack has been forbidden by his superior at the Yard to go after statements like that?'

'I'm not Uncle Jack, am I?' she replied defiantly. 'I met most of those women after they'd been released, some of them still sick with the consequences of being force-fed, and the ones I didn't actually get to meet were interviewed by Emmeline Pethick-Lawrence.'

'Do you still have those statements?'

'Of course, but how could I pass them over to Uncle Jack without him knowing how I got them, or who put them into a generalised form suitable for publication?'

'You obviously can't,' Percy said thoughtfully, 'but I'm going to ask you to be very brave and admit to him who you are, and give him those statements, in the hope that the ladies concerned would be willing to make the same allegations on oath in a court of law.'

'Of *course* they would!' Annabelle insisted. 'They'd be only too glad to get their ordeals exposed for what they were, and see the perpetrators brought to justice.'

'Excellent!' Percy murmured. 'So here's what we do. I'll make arrangements to come up to Watford — perhaps on the excuse of another family lunch — and get you and your Uncle Jack into a quiet corner, where you can make your confession, which I all but guarantee will be greeted with glowing thanks when you hand over those statements.'

'I hope you're right,' Annabelle said, shuddering. 'I owe him *so* much, along with Aunt Esther, and I've been feeling like a traitor every time I write one of my articles. But I'm determined to see justice done.'

'So is Jack, and so am I,' Percy assured her, then leaned forward and pecked her on the cheek. 'I'm secretly very proud of you, Annabelle, even though you chose a very hazardous way of earning that pride. Now wipe that tear from your eye; for one thing it might freeze in this weather, and for another Lily just landed on her bottom.'

'What do you think Percy's up to this time?' Esther asked as they left the kitchen, having assured Polly the cook that it was fine to serve the roast lamb with minted potatoes, rather than the mash that she'd first considered.

'What makes you think that Uncle Percy's up to *anything*?' Jack asked.

'Mainly because he's Uncle Percy, and the family lunch was his idea,' Esther replied with a knowing smile. 'If he's just after a free feed, and blessed relief from Aunt Beattie's cooking, why ask me to invite Lucy and Teddy as well, so that there'll be less food to go round?'

'No doubt all will be revealed in due course,' Jack said, 'but now that the weather's eased somewhat, he no doubt wants to get out of Hackney for a day. And it's the least we can do after his generosity towards Lily and Annabelle, even if they did ruin their dresses on that ice.'

Esther looked up at the hall clock. 'It's almost eleven, and if they take their normal trains they'll be here within the hour. I must go upstairs and get properly dressed.'

Fifteen minutes later the front door bell rang, and Alice the maid scuttled down the hallway to open it. In the doorway stood Percy and Beattie, and as Jack came out of the sitting room with a look of surprise, Percy said, 'We took a special train that's been laid on to take people to Manchester for some sporting event or other, and the first stop was Watford. Hope we're not inconveniencing you?'

'No, not at all,' Jack assured him. 'Come into the sitting room, and I'll pour you a whisky and soda.'

'Spoken like a gentleman,' Percy said, grinning, then turned to Beattie. 'Why don't you go and watch Polly in the kitchen, dear? She can actually cook.'

Beattie departed with a snort of outrage, and Jack laughed. 'You're obviously feeling very brave this morning. You look rather pleased with yourself.'

'And with good cause,' Percy told him, 'since we may now each see a light at the end of our respective tunnels.'

'You've found this Pickford bloke?' Jack asked.

'In a manner of speaking. But we'll both need that whisky before I descend into detail.'

They were alone in the sitting room as Jack poured them both a whisky and soda, then looked eagerly across at Percy. 'Well?' he demanded. 'You obviously contrived this meeting in order to impart something important in private, and now's your chance. Beattie's in the kitchen, Esther's upstairs putting her face on, and Teddy and Lucy haven't arrived yet. So tell me how you tracked down Pickford, then show me "the light at the end of my tunnel", as you put it.'

'In reverse order,' Percy said, smirking as he rose from the armchair and left the sitting room, leaving Jack puzzled. He heard the telltale creak of the third stair leading to the upper storey, and wondered why Percy had taken this moment, of all moments, to visit the bathroom. Then he heard the same creak again, plus a faint rustling sound, and Percy re-entered the sitting room carrying a bundle of papers.

'You mentioned that Barrymore forbade you from collecting statements from Suffragettes let down by the matron system,' he began. 'But what if those statements were supplied to you without any effort on your part?'

'Is that what you have in your hand?' Jack demanded with mounting excitement. 'Stop imitating a theatrical conjuror and hand them over — *now*!'

'To hear is to obey,' Percy said, passing him the papers, and Jack eagerly read the first of the statements, then ran his eyes over the other four in order to make sure that they were of the same nature. Each of them named a police station, a date, and a Suffragette, and gave sickening detail regarding the ordeal that they'd undergone, along with a further assertion that when they'd tried to lodge a complaint regarding what had happened with a matron, they'd received responses along the lines of 'it's not my business', or 'you must have done something to lead him on', or 'shut up, or you'll get worse.'

'This is potentially explosive stuff,' Jack said as he looked back across at Percy, 'but it's all in the same handwriting, and none of these complaints is signed. I can't present them to Barrymore like this. And actually, this handwriting is vaguely familiar...'

'So it should be.' Percy nodded towards Jack's empty glass. 'You're going to need that refilled in just a moment,' he assured him, then walked to the sitting room door and flung it open.

'You can come in now,' he told the person waiting in the hallway, and into the sitting room walked a pale-faced Annabelle.

'Meet Anthony Pickford,' Percy announced, as the whisky glass slid from Jack's fingers.

## CHAPTER FOURTEEN

'I really didn't mean to show you any disrespect, or bring disgrace on the family that adopted me,' Annabelle assured Jack in the smallest voice he'd ever heard her employ. 'It's just that these women need a voice, and I wanted to use my gift for a good cause.'

'You'll have to give me a chance to take all this in,' Jack replied hoarsely. 'I've just discovered that someone I love like a daughter has been playing a dangerous political game, and risking being locked away for many years. Please don't tell me that your only reason for doing it was in order to get your writing published.'

'It probably was, at first,' Annabelle conceded. 'But when I learned what these women were being subjected to, something hardened inside me, and when the Government refused to even listen to demands for equality, then set about allowing the women to be physically abused merely for speaking out, well, that was what you might call the "final straw". I realised that I could help them in my own small way.'

'I'd hardly call it a "small way",' Jack replied. 'You seem to have become the chosen mouthpiece for half the population, and exposed the current Government for what it is. If it makes you feel any better, I've been trying to persuade my superior inside Scotland Yard to let me investigate what's been going on in some police stations. Not the force-feeding in prisons, of course, but the physical assaults in cells, since they *are* in a sense within my area of responsibility. One half of me wants to congratulate you for your courage, talent and determination, and the other half wants to call you impetuous, stubborn, foolhardy and rebellious. At present, I think the good half's winning.'

'So you aren't going to throw me out?' Annabelle asked nervously.

'Of *course* I'm not. We love you, and I for one am proud of you. Come here and give me a big hug.'

As they stood with their arms around each other, tears running down their cheeks, Percy gave a polite cough.

'There is, of course, a massive benefit to be gained from all this,' he announced, and when Annabelle and Jack disengaged from their hug and looked at him enquiringly, he added, 'Those statements that Annabelle obtained from women assaulted in their cells — they're the perfect ammunition for approaching Barrymore with a demand for an end to the farcical pretence that makes it all possible. Put another way, the termination of the matron system.'

'He'd never agree to that, even in the face of all the evidence,' Jack insisted. 'He's only interested in demonstrating that we have a system in place, not in proving that it actually works. His political masters in the Home Office would be unforgiving if he went to them with the feeble admission that what seemed like a good idea has been the means by which the very opposite outcome has been achieved. Women in police cells are not being protected by matrons — it's the matrons who're making it possible for them to be abused.'

'But supposing that you suggested another layer of supervision?' Percy suggested. 'We keep the matron system for appearances' sake, but we have them supervised by a new, higher authority that's beyond moral challenge or possible corruption. Female, preferably, but drawn from impeccable areas of society, such as the churches, the hospitals or even the universities.'

'Clearly that would allow Barrymore and his like to save face, and perhaps even make themselves appear like reformers for the good of women,' Jack agreed, 'but we'd need to be certain that the women employed have the moral courage and the force of personality to ensure adequate reform and supervision of the matrons.'

'Well, I'm married to one,' Percy said with a chuckle, and it fell silent for a moment before Annabelle added her opinion.

'What Uncle Percy's suggesting makes admirable sense, Uncle Jack. No-one argues with Aunt Beattie — except perhaps Uncle Percy, and he normally comes off second-best. If you can persuade your superior to implement such a system, I could write articles praising the Government's far-sightedness and concern for the rights of female prisoners, which would not only garner support for the new regime, but would also make your superior feel that he'd achieved something worthwhile in the eyes of those who matter to him. That's assuming that you aren't going to forbid me writing more articles.'

'Before Jack answers that,' Percy interrupted, 'there's something you should both know. I began my search for Anthony Pickford at the offices of the *Daily Mail*, whose news editor, a Mr. Bentinck, asked me to advise Pickford that whatever the outcome of my enquiries, there is a permanent job for him on the staff of the *Daily Mail*.'

'But he didn't know that Pickford is a woman,' Annabelle pointed out.

Percy laughed. 'Then he's in for a considerable surprise, is he not? And Jack, let me remind you of the great advantages to be gained from having someone on the inside of everything. Over to you.'

'I wouldn't dream of telling you to abandon your writing,' Jack told Annabelle, 'but you'll have to forgive me if I keep it a secret between ourselves. The shock would be too much for your Aunt Esther, I fear, and as for Aunt Beattie — well, I'll leave that to your fertile imagination.'

'Thank you *so* much, Uncle Jack!' Annabelle beamed as she leaned forward and kissed him on the cheek. 'I won't let you down, I promise! Now, with your permission, I'll take my lunch in my room along with Lily, then we'd planned to go walking in the park, before the last of the snow thaws away. It's so beautiful out there, with those rolling acres of white, and the animals huddling for shelter together under the trees.'

Once the door had closed behind her, Jack sat down heavily and took a long slug of whisky and soda, then smiled ruefully at Percy. 'Any more rude shocks, or is two your quota for today?'

'What was the second shock?'

'The realisation that you were ahead of me in working out where to go next. We — by which, of course, I probably mean "I" — must persuade Barrymore that the matron system isn't working, then suggest a new supervisory scheme maintained and operated by formidable ladies such as Aunt Beattie.'

'She'll be the first to sign up,' Percy assured him. 'She left herself wide open on Boxing Day, when she asked you to let her know if you came up with some way of further protecting women in custody. If Beattie weren't so damned straight-laced, crusty and religiously inclined, she'd be the first manning the barricades at these rallies and demonstrations hosted by the Suffragettes. She probably practises female equality as avidly as most of them. If we can convince her that forming a group of God-fearing, tight-corseted old battleaxes who'll make sure that women are not attacked while in police custody is her life's calling, then she'll be ideal for the job.'

'Well, you can have the formidable task of persuading her,' Jack said with a grimace, then cocked an ear towards sounds of greeting from the front hall. 'That sounds like Lucy and Teddy arriving, so let's go and be sociable, shall we?'

They had just made it to the front hall when they were spotted by Esther, who was descending the staircase.

'You might have been here to welcome your own sister and her husband,' she said, frowning at Jack, while Alice was in the process of taking the hats, coats and gloves from the latest arrivals into the rear parlour. 'Instead, you were knocking back whisky with your partner in crime.'

'We were putting the world to rights,' Jack explained, 'as you shall hear once we get to the tea and muffins stage. For the time being, let's all go into the sitting room and make inroads into our drinks cabinet.'

'Are you *sure* they don't suspect me of something as well?' Lily asked fearfully as she walked alongside Annabelle up the main drive of Cassiobury Park.

'Your name didn't even come up in the conversation,' Annabelle hastened to reassure her. 'I think your father was too stunned by what he'd learned about me for it to occur to him that you might have strayed from the straight and narrow as well. So you can continue with your training in what I believe they call "first aid". How's it coming on?'

'There's more to it than that,' Lily told her. 'Nursing requires those who practise it to know as much as doctors, if not more, about how the human body works. When we meet with Sarah Millichip to learn those skills we're likely to need as medical orderlies in the cause, she encourages me to stay back afterwards and learn more advanced stuff that I'll probably never need to put into practice, particularly since that new Home Secretary doesn't seem quite so keen to take us on. In fact, it's rumoured that he's considering offering Suffragettes in prison political status, so that should put an end to the hunger strikes. It also means we'll have less reason to stage protests, so the chances are that my skills won't be called upon quite so regularly in the future. But in the meantime, I'm learning all that I can about nursing.'

'So we're both doing what we want to do,' Annabelle said happily, 'except I'm doing it with your father's blessing, although it's being kept secret from Aunt Esther. But from what you say, there won't even be anything for me to write about. I won't say that I'll be disappointed if the Suffragettes get all that they're campaigning for, but it'll certainly deprive me of subject matter.'

'I'm sure you'll think of something,' Lily assured her. 'And it's such exciting news that you've been offered a job at the *Daily Mail*!'

'It's actually Anthony Pickford who's been offered the job,' Annabelle reminded her, 'and so far as I'm aware, the *Daily Mail* doesn't employ a single female writer.'

'So how have you been "putting the world to rights", as you boasted before lunch?' Esther asked Jack. They were in the sitting room, and the conversation had begun to flag as the large lunch they'd just consumed started to make everyone drowsy.

'It's really Percy's idea,' Jack hedged, staring meaningfully at Percy, who gave a little shrug as he took the cue.

'I think I know how to ensure that women, and other vulnerable people, taken into police custody can be properly protected against abuse and downright unlawful assaults,' he announced.

'About time someone did,' Beattie growled. 'But didn't Jack say that his superiors were not convinced that the system needs reforming?'

'He did,' Percy confirmed, 'but Jack now has the evidence to justify his claim that improvements are required.'

'Only improvements?' Teddy queried. 'Surely, if the system's as rotten as Jack's led us to believe, then you need to close it down completely and replace it with something else. In the building trade, you don't construct a house on poor foundations — you take out those foundations and begin again.'

'That's where the problem lies, as I also explained on Boxing Day,' Jack put in. 'The powers that be in the Met daren't admit that they constructed a system that was almost guaranteed to fail, because the very people installed in order to guard the vulnerable were equally vulnerable themselves. Any new system has to allow those who'll be called upon to implement it to save face.'

'So what have you come up with?' Teddy persisted.

'Another, higher, level of supervision and monitoring,' Percy replied. 'One that ensures that the matrons currently in place are not deflected from their purpose by bribery or threats.'

'More men in positions of authority over women?' Beattie objected. 'The one aspect of the matron system that met with my approval was that it was staffed by women.'

'But women who were open to corruption, not because they were women, but because of their connection with the very men whose actions they were intended to control,' Percy pointed out. 'The system I have in mind would involve the appointment of overseers whose moral integrity and courage are beyond question, and cannot be polluted or compromised. Women who can set the standard for all women in their actions, judgments, and adherence to the Christian way of life.'

'And where do you intend to find those?' Esther asked doubtfully.

Percy smiled like a successful concert pianist at the end of a performance as he declared, 'I found the first on Boxing Day.'

Esther's eyes opened wider, then she burst out laughing. 'She was only expressing an interest in preserving the welfare of women in custody, not volunteering to become the sergeant major of some "Moral Rectitude Army". Isn't that so, Aunt Beattie?'

Beattie looked perplexed as all eyes turned to her, and she asked, 'What did I say, exactly?'

'I made a special note of your precise words at the time,' Percy oozed, 'since I was so proud to be married to you. What you actually said, when Jack announced that he was hoping to introduce a regime under which women who are not easily corrupted were placed in charge of the guardianship of women in custody, was, "Well, when you do, let me know." We have, and we're now letting you know. The ball just landed on your side of the court, my dear.'

'Splendid!' Teddy exclaimed as he clapped his hands in appreciation. 'Heaven defend any wicked constable seeking to take advantage of a vulnerable woman when Beattie Enright's around!'

Beattie's face expressed her confusion, but gave little indication of indecision as she asked Percy, 'What exactly have you in mind, you incorrigible schemer?'

'An elite group of women of the highest moral character, drawn from revered institutions such as the Church, whose task will be to visit those police stations in which matrons have been installed, to examine the cell records, interview prisoners to ensure that there have been no grounds for complaint, supervise the roster of matrons, then report direct to the Home Secretary's Office to share their findings.'

'And what role did you envisage for me in all this?' Beattie asked.

'Who better than yourself to set the standard by being the first to be appointed?' Percy enthused. 'The Florence Nightingale of the police cells, shining her lamp of moral rectitude into the darkest corners, and bringing the light of God's good grace to bear in the shadows that might otherwise be occupied by the servants of Satan.'

'Perhaps *you* should be writing for the *Daily Mail*,' Esther observed with a wry smile, 'and at least for once it wasn't me who walked over your trapdoor. What did Shakespeare call it, Lucy? "Hoist by one's own petard"?'

'That's from *Hamlet*,' Jack replied. 'I remember it well, since Uncle Percy persuaded me to join Lucy's theatre group using a similar strategy to the one with which he just persuaded Aunt Beattie to strike a blow for the safety of women in custody.'

'I don't recall agreeing to do it,' Beattie objected, to soft jeers and catcalls around the sitting room.

'If you do it, I will,' Lucy announced, 'whether Teddy approves or not.'

All eyes turned to Esther, who tried to excuse herself. 'I have a school to run,' she pointed out.

However, Jack reminded her of her reaction on Boxing Day when he'd pointed out that those in peril in police custody were not just Suffragettes, but young girls like Lily and Annabelle, arrested simply for being in the wrong place at the wrong time.

'I don't have a choice, do I?' Esther conceded, and the three men clapped their hands.

'Three cheers for the Beatrice Enright Morality Regiment!' Teddy called out.

'If I must become involved in this latest scheme by my husband, then at least let's dignify it with a better name than that,' Beattie insisted. 'The ball's back in *your* court, genius.' She glared at Percy.

There was a moment's indecision, then Percy responded, 'Since these new campaigners for the safety of women in custody will be visiting police stations, and since they will almost certainly be drawn from that stratum of society occupied by true ladies, why not "lady visitors"?'

'That's certainly better than what Teddy called us,' Beatrice nodded, 'and I propose that we hold our first meeting over a fresh pot of tea, while the menfolk leave us in peace.'

Jack was steeling himself for the task of attempting to persuade Chief Superintendent Barrymore of the need for 'lady visitors' when he was pre-empted by the sudden appearance of the man himself in his office doorway.

'Have you been secretly handing scandalous rubbish to the popular newspapers?' he demanded.

Jack was able to look suitably offended by the suggestion. 'Most certainly not, sir, but might I ask what makes you think that I have?'

'The latest drivel by the more pernicious of the guttersnipes they employ — a clod called Pickford, who's claiming to have spoken with Suffragette types who were handled inappropriately by police officers in various police stations, including Bow Street.'

'Does he cite names — of the victims, I mean?' Jack asked.

Barrymore shook his head. 'No. Like the coward he is, he simply drops the innuendo, implying that he could name names, but refusing to do so.'

'You will recall my raising with you, fairly recently, the rumours that were circulating to the effect that the matron system was flawed, and that the murder of that one attached to Bow Street had been carried out to silence her,' Jack reminded him. 'Your response, as I recall, was that we — meaning I — should do nothing to weaken the peoples' faith in the system that we'd implemented, even if it might have certain failings.'

'That's why I asked if you'd gone behind my back, stirring the pot,' Barrymore retorted as he stepped over the threshold and occupied Jack's visitor seat without invitation. 'You weren't happy to leave it at that, clearly.'

'And I didn't,' Jack told him. 'Instead, it occurred to me that there was a simple means to maintain the existing system, while at the same time reinforcing it so as to quash any suggestion that it wasn't doing the job it was intended to do.'

'And what have you come up with?' Barrymore asked suspiciously.

'Nothing too revolutionary,' Jack replied with a reassuring smile. 'A sort of supervisory committee composed of ladies of impeccable moral character, who will report regularly to the Home Secretary that the system is working the way it was intended.'

'And if it's not?'

'Then the ladies in question will instigate the necessary changes. All that will be required will be for them to be given the necessary authority.'

'Would this require the intervention of the Commissioner, do you think?'

'Probably only the Assistant Commissioner.'

'And how do you foresee them carrying out their duties?' Barrymore asked.

'They visit those police stations in which matrons have been employed, checking first-hand that the cell records reflect the true position, and enquiring of female and other vulnerable prisoners whether they've been properly treated. They then report their findings to the Assistant Commissioner. He, in turn, will report regularly to the Home Secretary.'

'How can you be sure that these new supervisors will not themselves become corrupted?'

'We will appoint the leading lights of churches, hospitals, universities and so on — ladies so far above the grubby reality of activities within police cells, and those who conduct them, that they can never be accused of bias, partiality or corruption.'

'And you have identified some such ladies?' Barrymore asked disbelievingly.

'I have indeed,' Jack assured him, 'and the first three are ready to assume responsibilities. I've selected a senior member of a respected Methodist Mission congregation in north-east London, supported by a school headmistress and a Holborn socialite highly regarded for her contributions to the arts.'

'Very well, leave it with me,' Barrymore instructed him, then turned to go, before stopping, turning back and enquiring, 'Have you given this new organisation a name?'

'They've done that for us, sir, and wish to be known as "lady visitors".'

'Very well, "lady visitors" it shall be. But don't let them loose until I've got the approval of Assistant Commissioner Macready.'

'No, sir,' Jack agreed, then allowed himself a smile as he contemplated the prospect of Aunt Beattie waging a moral campaign that would turn the Metropolitan Police inside out.

*

'It's very good of you to see us,' Emmeline smiled at *Daily Mail* news editor Samuel Bentinck as she and Annabelle took the visitor's seats into which he waved them.

'I agreed to see *you*, certainly,' Bentinck replied, 'given our long — well, "collaboration" is probably the word. But who's this?' He inclined his head towards Annabelle.

'You asked to meet Anthony Pickford, did you not?'

'I did, but who's she? Can she lead me to Mr Pickford?'

'She *is* Mr Pickford,' Emmeline told him triumphantly, taking great pleasure in watching Bentinck's mouth opening and closing like a stranded fish.

'But … but…' was all he managed before Annabelle giggled and completed the sentence for him.

'But I'm just a woman — well spotted, Mr Bentinck.'

'Is this some sort of bad joke?' Bentinck asked Emmeline.

'Am I famed for my sense of humour?' she retorted.

'So this — this young lady has been producing all that wonderful copy that you've been supplying me with?'

'Indeed she has,' Emmeline confirmed.

Bentinck frowned. 'Prove it,' he demanded, sliding a sheet of paper across the desk towards Annabelle. 'Here's a brief story just in from one of our East End stringers, all about the eviction of a widow and two children from a tenement in Wapping late yesterday. And here's a pen and some paper — give it the Anthony Pickford touch.'

Annabelle read the brief item, pursed her lips thoughtfully, then began writing, while Bentinck and Emmeline engaged in general conversation.

'Your paper's been very quiet of late,' Bentinck observed.

Emmeline nodded. 'Things have quietened down considerably since Mr Churchill become Home Secretary. He seems to have appreciated that he'll get nowhere simply by using brute force and attracting critical comment from the likes of you and I. There's even a rumour that he's prepared to concede political status to our crusaders for women's equality. If so, there won't be any more hunger strikes, with their appalling Government responses. So it begins to look as if we're getting somewhere at long last.'

'That won't suit me, of course,' Bentinck said, 'since I rely on you lot to give me the ringing headlines from yet another window-smashing excursion, or another invasion of the Parliamentary Chamber.'

'That's your problem,' Emmeline told him. 'Mine is the real prospect that without the Suffragettes' need for a news broadsheet, I may be seeking another livelihood.'

Annabelle looked up from what she'd been writing, and slipped the paper back across the desk. Bentinck's eyes opened wide in appreciation as he read what she had written:

*The depths of the winter chill may have retreated from the streets of the East End, but it clearly still lives on in the heart of the superintendent of Loxley's Dwellings at 37, Mill Yard in Wapping, where yesterday the neighbours were treated — if that is the apt word to employ — to the heart-rending sight of twenty-eight-year-old widow Clara Townsend clutching her sobbing children as they stood in the street, surrounded by their few pathetic possessions, after being evicted without warning because the rent was two days overdue. Clara was recently widowed when her coal-heaver husband was buried in a sudden cargo slide in the Albert Docks, and in vain did her horrified neighbours plead with the superintendent to take the few outstanding pence from them in order that Clara might retain the roof over her head. The reason? The heartless owners have another tenant lined up for their single-room hovel — one who's prepared to pay a shilling more a week. Nothing could be colder than the heart of a landlord, and we must question what our society has come to.*

'You clearly have an eye for the human tragedy,' Bentinck muttered in muted admiration, 'and you may be able to bring alive an idea that's been lurking inside my head for some time now. We national dailies are constantly criticised for not offering a female perspective in our headline stories, and we could perhaps attract a sizeable number of women readers if we were to begin publishing "The Lady's Point of View". How would you like to be that "Lady"?' He smiled at Annabelle. When she looked a little reluctant, he added, 'Eight shillings a week, and I'll make arrangements for you to have your own little cubby hole down the hall there, away from prying male eyes.'

'It's just that my parents don't know what I've been up to these past few months,' Annabelle admitted. 'They think I'm studying in a library near Euston, so I could only be here five days a week, between ten and three.'

'That doesn't concern me,' Bentinck said. 'You must have been writing somewhere in secret as Anthony Pickford, and provided that you can show up here regularly with writing of that quality, I don't care if you're based on a barge on the Thames. So will you come and work for me?'

'With the greatest of pleasure,' Annabelle replied. 'You just made my fondest dream come true. And you may rest assured that the *Daily Mail* will soon have a lot more women readers. But I can't use my own name, clearly. How about "Constance Bradley"?'

'Welcome to the *Daily Mail*, Constance Bradley,' Bentinck said as he held out his hand to shake.

'And thank you for striking yet another blow for female equality within the professional world,' Emmeline added, beaming.

# CHAPTER FIFTEEN

As soon as Jack reported that the Assistant Commissioner had given his approval for the formation of The League of Lady Visitors, Beattie sprang into action with an energy that belied her advancing years. She immediately appointed herself the Chief Superintendent and held her first meeting the following Sunday afternoon in the front parlour of her Hackney home, from which Percy was exiled to the garden for its duration. The meeting was attended by Esther, Lucy, and two senior ladies from the Hackney Methodist Mission of which Beattie was also a leading figure, encouraged by a minister who saw an opportunity to shed the light of God's forgiveness and mercy into the dark corners of London life.

By the end of a month, there were almost twenty lady visitors, as the word spread that there was missionary work to be done among the poor and despairing of the nation's capital. It was therefore perhaps inevitable that the visitors became known within selected Metropolitan Police stations as 'religious cranks' whose primary objective was to convert the Godless confined within their cells. However, the police were also well aware that these formidable ladies came with the authority of the Home Secretary, and were more than determined to put a stop to any form of abuse of female prisoners by those who held the cell keys.

The women in the cells were not all Suffragettes. In fact, as 1910 progressed, there were fewer of them evident even in the streets, which meant fewer of them were arrested. The women under the protection of Beattie and her warriors for morality were therefore not solely middle-class crusaders for female emancipation, but also prostitutes, street drunks and petty thieves. Whatever punishment was awaiting them at the hands of the magistrates was preceded by homilies from women more fortunate than themselves on how to deport themselves as wives, mothers and representatives of their sex once they were back out on the streets.

The introduction of the lady visitor programme brought a sudden end to assaults in the cells. Beattie and her disciples had come down heavily against the offenders on the first few occasions on which such behaviour had been brought to their attention, and had insisted that it be dealt with at the very least by disciplinary action, and in the worst cases by criminal prosecution. The matrons who'd been covering up such wrongdoing soon learned that their services could swiftly be dispensed with following an adverse report from a lady visitor, and by the summer of that year there were no more allegations of cell rapes or indecent assaults in hallways. But this had the effect of shifting the location of such attacks, which were now being inflicted on female prisoners either in alleyways adjacent to where they were apprehended, or in covered police wagons taking them to the station. Clearly, more work still needed to be done to protect such women.

The reduction in Suffragette activity was due in large part to a seeming change of heart by the new Home Secretary, Winston Churchill, which was really only a change in policy. He was recorded expressing the private opinion that, 'Once you give votes to the vast number of women who form the majority of the community, all power passes to their hands,' which was, of course, at the same time a strong argument in favour of precisely *why* they should be enfranchised.

The more militant of Emmeline Pankhurst's followers had ceased taking on police officers in street confrontations, and had now adopted the habit of chaining themselves to things — frequently railings — in order to publicise their cause. Hearing of this, Churchill observed, 'I might as well chain myself to St Thomas's Hospital and say I would not move till I had had a baby.' However, for largely political reasons, he introduced Rule 243A, which allowed improved conditions in gaol for those Suffragettes who had not been convicted of any serious offence. The hunger strikes ceased overnight.

The underlying reason for this apparent change of sentiment was that at the turn of the year, Asquith's Government had lost votes in a General Election, and was obliged to rely, in House debates, on the support of the forty-two Members returned by the rapidly growing Labour Party. In the belief that the die-hard Liberal opponents of votes for women might be manipulated towards a compromise, left-wing journalist Henry Brailsford brokered a suggestion that Emmeline Pankhurst exchange militancy for diplomacy and offer to host a Conciliation Committee, containing Members of Parliament and female suffrage campaigners who between them could negotiate a settlement of the long-standing dispute. She accepted, as did thirty-six sitting Members, and while the Conciliation Committee was meeting Pankhurst called off her troops, and there was no more disorder on the streets.

The temporary halt to confrontations between Suffragettes and police officers resulted in redundancy for those who had gathered around Sarah Millichip in order to learn how to minister as medical orderlies. This, in turn, led to an inevitable reduction in the numbers of those attending her weekly first aid classes in her neatly appointed apartments in Grimston

Road, Fulham. But a few remained in whom Sarah had engendered an interest in nursing skills, and Lily Enright was one of the most enthusiastic.

She was the last one remaining late one Thursday morning when Sarah invited her to stay on for a sandwich and a cup of tea. As they sat on opposite sides of Sarah's neat kitchen table, she raised an eyebrow and asked, 'You weren't just interested in holding smelling salts under noses, or splinting broken legs, were you? Your interest goes much deeper than that.'

'I'd really like to become a nurse like you,' Lily admitted.

Sarah smiled. 'I do believe that the same desire to help others in need of medical intervention that clearly inspires you is the one I first felt when I went through my training all those years ago. I'll never be allowed to return to it, now that my name's been blackened as a troublemaker, so you can imagine how frustrated I feel, not being allowed to employ all that I've learned. Would you let me teach you, if only to get this nagging urge out of my head?'

'I'd love that,' Lily enthused, 'and I'd be willing to pay.'

'Nonsense, you'd be doing me a favour,' Sarah insisted, then thought briefly before enquiring, 'Would you like to learn how to bring someone back from the dead?'

'Is that possible?' Lily asked. 'If so, why did the Bible make such a fuss about it when our Lord did that for Lazarus?'

'Bless you, girl,' Sarah said with chuckle, 'I wasn't talking about the resurrection of someone who's clinically dead. But it's possible to bring someone back when they're on the brink of death because their heart's stopped briefly, and they've ceased breathing. There's a brief moment when you can resuscitate them, as it's called, by literally breathing the life back into them. Go and fetch Millie and I'll show you.'

Millie was a full-size window display mannequin that had been devoted to the cause the previous year, and which Sarah had employed in order to demonstrate skills such as splinting broken limbs and stemming blood flows. Millie was naked, and made of wax, which made it easier to bend her limbs in a realistic portrayal of how the same actions could be performed on live patients. Lily had long since ceased to be embarrassed by the sight of her pallid nakedness. She put down the remains of her sandwich, went into the rear room in which Sarah normally conducted her lessons, and came back with the pasty-looking lady in question.

'First of all, lay her on her back and tilt her head to the left,' Sarah instructed Lily, who did as requested.

'Now you have to pretend that her mouth can be opened,' came the next instruction, 'so pretend to open it, then look inside to make sure that there's no obstruction, like a tongue or a lump of food. If so, remove it or push it to one side.'

Feeling slightly foolish over the pretence, Lily went through the motions, then looked back up enquiringly for further instruction.

'Now pinch the nose firmly, and blow into the open mouth five times with heavy breaths of your own,' Sarah said, adding, 'It'll feel funny on Millie because her mouth's closed, but with a real person you'll feel it going down their throat. Then you remove your own mouth, take a deep breath and do it again. Repeat that as often as necessary until you feel some response from the patient, such as them suddenly catching their own breath or opening their eyes. Sometimes you have to get out of the way if they suddenly start to vomit — that's one reason why you have to turn their head to the side when you commence the procedure.'

'Ugh!' Lily recoiled. 'And even if they don't, it can't be all that hygienic, can it? And some people have — you know — bad breath, don't they?'

'The price you pay for being a nurse,' Sarah replied. 'The reward is the feeling you get when they come back to life.'

'Even so,' Lily said, grimacing,' I can't ever imagine a situation in which I'd be doing it, but thank you anyway.'

Emmeline and her colleagues were not entirely satisfied with what the Conciliation Committee had finally come up with, but it set a valuable precedent, and it moved the long-term agenda in the right direction. Its greatest strategic failure in the eyes of many was that it linked voting rights to property ownership and/or married status.

Specifically, the rights would be given to all women who owned 'real property' — land or buildings — valued at ten pounds or more, or who were married to men with such property. But since it was an achievement of sorts, and would give the vote to over one million British women, the Suffragette members of the Committee agreed to it being placed on the Parliamentary calendar, where it was carried by over a hundred votes in its Second Reading in the Commons in July.

Then disaster struck when it was sent to the Committee stage, and Labour Party leader Keir Hardie requested a two-hour time allocation for debate. Then, for some inexplicable reason, Prime Minister Asquith withdrew it from the Parliamentary agenda, while announcing his intention to have the current Parliament dissolved at the end of November, ahead of another general election.

Emmeline Pankhurst was both stunned and appalled by the betrayal, and issued a call to arms that was rapidly relayed through the secret communication channels that had become well established over the years. She resisted the temptation to call for early retribution, instead making detailed long-term plans designed to lull Asquith into the false belief that the dust had settled on his treachery.

Lily was one of the first to know what was being plotted, since all that was required in her case was a note left for her at the front counter of the Reading Room in the British Museum Library that she and Annabelle were still visiting daily. Annabelle was in fact composing her regular pieces for the *Daily Mail*, seated at her usual desk, then slipping away for the omnibus ride to their offices in order to hand her offering over to be typewritten, edited, and sent to the composition room. Given that there had been no recent flare-ups on the Suffragette battlelines, her more recent pieces had focused on other women's issues, such as the total lack of any compensation, or other material support, for widows left with large families to rear after the early death of a husband. Such deaths were frequently caused by accidents in factories, on building sites, or on the docks. She also took a swipe at the prevalence of domestic violence inflicted by men on their wives and children, and the seeming indifference of the prosecuting authorities when these appalling breaches of trust were courageously reported by their victims.

When told by Lily that there was to be another mass protest inside Parliament House, Annabelle made arrangements to be there, after visiting the intended target several times and assessing where she might best position herself to view the action and send a first-hand account of it to her editor. Lily, meanwhile, prepared to put her first aid skills into practice once more.

Prime Minister Asquith had other matters on his mind as he struggled to gain the necessary support for his Chancellor Lloyd George's 'Peoples' Budget', and was therefore not well disposed to receiving a delegation of some three hundred angry Suffragists led by Emmeline Pankhurst following a meeting in Caxton Hall. Annabelle had followed discreetly behind the initial delegation, and was present when Emmeline received the terse refusal of Asquith to meet with her, delivered by a stern-faced doorman guarding the entrance to the Commons. Refusing to give in, she organised her troops to attempt to enter in small groups of twelve.

What happened next was recorded by Annabelle on the front page of the following day's *Daily Mail* in words partly contributed by Emmeline Pankhurst, and partly of her own making. Below the glaring headline, 'The Death of Democracy', Annabelle wrote a scathing condemnation of what she'd witnessed:

*As, one after the other, small deputations of twelve women appeared in sight, they were set upon by the police and hurled aside. Mrs Cobden Sanderson, who had been in the first deputation, was rudely seized and pressed against the wall by the police, who held her there by both arms for a considerable time, sneering and jeering at her. Then I saw that brave pioneer of the hunger strike, Miss Ada Wright, close to the entrance. Whether or not she was recognised by the police, they nevertheless seized her, lifted her from the ground and flung her back into the crowd. A moment later she appeared again, in a vain effort to gain entry to the House, running as fast as she could towards its entrance. A policeman struck her with all his force, and she fell to the ground. It was a painful and degrading sight as, time after time, she bravely regained her feet, only to be knocked down again immediately. Finally, as she lay against the wall of the House of Lords, close to the Strangers' Entrance, a number of women, with pale and stressed faces, were kneeling down round her. She was in a state of collapse.*

*'It was a gallant but heartbreaking sight to see those little deputations battling against overwhelming odds, and then to see them torn asunder and scattered, bruised and battered, against the organised crowd of rowdies. I discovered, later, that those picked men of 'A Division' of the Metropolitan Police, who had always been called out on previous occasions, had this time been ordered to stick close to the House itself, while many of them remained in reserve at Bow Street Police Station. Those with whom the brave campaigners for women's justice came into contact had been brought in specially from outlying districts, which was both a cynical and a deliberate ploy. The men of A Division had come to know the Suffragists, to understand their aims and objectives, and therefore, while obeying their orders, they had come to treat the women, as far as possible, with courtesy and consideration. But these new men with whom the women had to deal yesterday — who, or so I was informed, had been drafted in from Whitechapel — were ignorant, ill-mannered, and of an entirely different type. They had nothing of the correct official manner, and were to be seen laughing and jeering at the women who they maltreated.'*

While all this mayhem had been occupying Annabelle's attention, Lily had been accompanying Sarah Millichip as they treated one casualty after another. Most of their patients were either severely bruised, or groggy from being battered around the head or thrown against the stone edifice of Parliament House with considerable force. A few broken limbs here and there, and the need for smelling salts, was the sum total of the demands made for their medical intervention. After instructing someone to summon an ambulance for the unconscious, but still breathing, Ada Wright, Sarah turned to Lily with a kindly smile.

'I think we're done for today, dear, and thank you for your experienced assistance.'

Lily was picking her way through the shattered battle banners of the WSPU, and the ripped and discarded green, purple and white sashes like the one draped across her chest, when she heard screams for assistance. They were coming from an alleyway to one side of the Members' Entrance that had seen so much of the fighting. A woman in her late thirties, smartly dressed and seemingly unharmed, was kneeling down beside the prostrate girl aged about eight or nine.

'For the love of God, someone help me!' the woman screamed. 'I think my precious Emily's dead!'

Lily raced over and knelt down beside the girl, who appeared not to be breathing, while the woman with her — presumably her mother — continued wailing, throwing her hands in the air and calling on God to come to her assistance.

'What happened?' Lily asked once the woman paused for breath.

'We were coming up from the common on the river side of the building,' the woman explained, 'and walking up this shortcut, when two hulking great policemen came down towards us, struggling with this large woman who was demanding votes for women. I tried to push Emily out of their way, but she got knocked sideways, into that wall. You can see the blood on her head, and I don't think she's breathing anymore. Can you help her?'

'I can try,' Lily replied, then knelt closer to confirm that the girl had indeed stopped breathing. Then her instincts and training kicked in, and she rolled the girl's head to the left, opened her lips, pinched her nose, and began blowing into her mouth. After five deep breaths she paused momentarily, and the women demanded to know what she was doing.

'Trying to restore her breathing,' Lily explained, then bent down again to her appointed task. After four more attempts, she became aware of the girl's eyes flickering, and felt the juddering under her neat little bodice as the breath surged back into her lungs. She sat back up in triumph as the girl's eyes opened fully. Then she caught sight of her mother and burst into tears.

'You're an angel from Heaven!' the mother declared, just as two burly police officers wearing the shoulder insignia of H Division of the Met, and therefore identifiable as coming from Whitechapel, came down the narrow alleyway towards them.

'There's one ripe fer the pickin',' one of them said to the other. Without a further word being spoken, they leaned down and scooped a startled Lily into the air, where she began kicking and screaming.

The woman with the recently resurrected child yelled in protest. 'She just saved my daughter's life! Leave her alone, you brutes!'

'Clear off!' one of them replied as he pulled Lily's sash forward for her to read more carefully. 'She's wearin' the battle colours o' that lot what we've bin sent ter take along ter Bow Street, so out the way, else you gets it an' all!'

With that he let the banner fall back onto Lily's chest, taking the opportunity to fondle her breasts with an appreciative grunt as he gave the word for his colleague to assist in carrying their prisoner up the alleyway towards a waiting police wagon.

Annabelle had enough notes for a dozen headline items as she made her way through the dwindling crowds and watched the last of the police wagons pulling away with their loads. Then she stared in horror as she turned her attention to the call of 'One more fer Bow Street!' Two grinning uniformed officers were carrying Lily to the open rear door of one of the last wagons and throwing her in alongside three others who'd already been roughly apprehended.

'Don't worry, Lily — I'll get help!' Annabelle shouted, uncertain whether or not she'd have heard her reassurance. But an idea came into her head almost immediately. She raced across Parliament Square to the cab rank, pressed coins into the cabman's hands and requested that he take her to the offices of the *Daily Mail* in Fleet Street.

From there, she made an urgent telephone call to Aunt Beattie, hoping that she wasn't too late.

# CHAPTER SIXTEEN

Beattie Enright swept into the large and noisy holding room inside Bow Street Police Station as if she owned the place, scanned it with a stern and enquiring gaze, then hurried over to where Lily was seated in crumpled clothing, looking both deflated and guilty.

'I'm sorry, Aunt Beattie,' she mumbled.

'Sorry for what, exactly?' Beattie demanded. 'Telling lies about how you've been spending all those days when you should have been studying in that library, or sorry for getting yourself arrested?'

'I didn't do *anything* to get myself arrested, honestly,' she insisted. 'I was just helping this little girl who was lying lifeless on the ground, when these two horrible brutes from Whitechapel, who have the cheek to call themselves guardians of the law, pulled me off the ground and threw me into a police wagon. As for studying in the library, I have been, *really* I have. I just want to be a nurse one day, and I've been learning all about it while coming to the assistance of women brutalised by police officers.'

'That no doubt explains that advertisement across your shoulders,' Beattie replied starchily as she read the words "Medical Orderly" on the sash that was still across Lily's torn bodice. 'And how did your clothing get ripped?'

'You wouldn't want to know,' Lily replied as she shook her head.

Just then, a large uniformed officer with sergeant's stripes on his tunic sleeves walked over and told Beattie, 'There's no talkin' ter prisoners, Missus, so I'd be obliged if yer'd leave this room so's we can process 'em.'

'I'm Beattie Enright,' she told him.

'Congratulations, and I'm Sergeant Logan, but I've never 'eard of yer.'

'But presumably you *have* heard of The League of Lady Visitors?'

'Them 'oly rollers, yer mean?'

'If you mean a group of dedicated ladies who're determined to bring Christian values to bear in ungodly places like this, then yes. I happen to be the founder and leader of that organisation, and we've put an end to more than one unsavoury practice inside many a police station, this one included. I'm surprised that our paths haven't crossed before.'

'Yer can stay 'til yer've satisfied yerself that this one ain't gonna cause any trouble, anyroad, although she don't look like one of them what's in need of bein' placed back on the straight an' narrow, an' off the streets.'

'She's my grandniece, you impudent wretch!' Beattie shouted. 'And so far as I can tell, her only "offence" was coming to the assistance of women left broken and bleeding by your thugs in uniform!'

'There she is!' came the triumphant voice of a woman who brushed past several constables in the doorway to bustle to Lily's side, then frown up at Sergeant Logan. 'This young woman saved the life of my precious daughter before she was rudely plucked from the street by two of your bullies. She's done no wrong, and I demand that she be released!'

'An' I s'pose she's *your* bloody grandniece an' all — that right?' Logan asked sarcastically, causing the woman to draw herself up to her full height and demand to know what justification the sergeant had for detaining Lily.

'I can't tell yer that,' Logan replied, 'since yer've got no authority in 'ere.'

'Young man,' the lady said, bristling, 'just so there's no further misunderstanding, my name is Emily Seely, and my husband — the father of the girl whose life was saved by this young lady less than two hours ago — is John Seely, Under-Secretary of State for the Colonies. He's about to take his rightful seat on the Privy Council. The current Home Secretary, Mr Churchill, has been a friend of his since the days when they were at Harrow together. Do you require any further evidence of my authority, and when are you going to release this young lady?'

'I'll need ter speak ter the inspector,' Logan mumbled as he crept away.

Emily Seely turned a beaming smile on Lily. 'Thank you once again, young lady, for your timely assistance. My daughter is the apple of my eye, and I'd like to reward you in some way. Since you're obviously a nurse, it would of course be unprofessional for me to offer you a financial sum, but...'

'She's *not* a nurse,' Beattie butted in, red in the face. 'She's my grandniece, and only got herself into this situation through her obsession with studying medicine.'

'That's true,' Lily admitted in a small voice. 'I'd *like* to be a nurse, but I don't think I'd be acceptable to any hospital now. I was just helping out when all those women were injured by rough handling from police officers.'

Emily Seely tilted her head and asked, 'Have you ever heard of the Nightingale Training School for Nurses?'

'Can't say I have,' Lily admitted.

'But you presumably *have* heard of Florence Nightingale?'

'Of course, since she's the most famous nurse that England's ever produced. But isn't she dead now?'

'She died only a few weeks ago, but her old family home was in Embley, which is in my husband's constituency, and our two families are quite friendly. The nursing school to which I referred was founded by Florence some fifty years ago, and is based in St Thomas's Hospital. Admission is eagerly sought after by cultured young ladies such as yourself; as a result, these days it's only achieved by personal recommendation. I'd be grateful if you'd let me recommend you as a reward for bringing dear little Emily back from the dead.'

Lily burst into tears, then nodded vigorously as she managed to burble, 'Oh, yes — yes, please!'

'What's wrong with Lily?' Lucy demanded of Beattie as she hurried into the room, adding, 'I came as fast as I could after you telephoned, but our carriage got held up in all that confusion that seems to have gripped the whole of Westminster. But why is Lily crying like that?'

'One of her dreams just came true,' Beattie said, smiling, 'although I'm not sure what your brother will make of all this. Which reminds me — have you seen Annabelle?'

'No, why?'

'Well, it was a telephone call from her that brought me down here in the first place, and I was wondering how she got to know what had happened.'

'Yer can all sling yer 'ook!' Sergeant Logan shouted as he reappeared in the doorway. 'The inspector's bin told as 'ow nobody's ter be charged, although God only knows why. So move yer arses, afore someone wiv some brains changes 'is mind fer 'im.'

As they made their way out into the large front entrance, Lily spotted Annabelle in one corner, talking earnestly to several women who looked as if they'd just emerged from a train wreck, while urgently writing things down in a notebook.

'Annabelle's just over there,' Lily told Beattie and Lucy, 'and if she's prepared to be as truthful as I've been, then our parents are in for a double shock.'

Once the initial surprise had worn off, Jack and Esther were proud of all that Lily and Annabelle had managed to achieve. However, they were less pleased when both young women revealed their plans to leave Watford to pursue their new careers in London. Percy and Beattie had offered to let them stay in their house in Hackney, so at least they would be safe and in familiar surroundings.

A few days after their daughters' shock announcement, Jack and Esther smiled bravely as the coach carrying Lily and Annabelle to their new home trundled out of the driveway and into Rickmansworth Road. They had far too much luggage between them to even consider travelling by train to Euston, and then by omnibus to Hackney. Despite their sadness at seeing them leave, Jack and Esther had realised that they were not children anymore and had to make their way in life. 'After all,' Esther said, 'I had to fend for myself when I was a few years younger than them, and that was in Spitalfields, which was — and probably still is — much rougher than Hackney.'

'At least they'll be maintaining a family tradition,' Jack replied, 'since I moved in with Uncle Percy and Aunt Beattie when I was fourteen, much to Mother's chagrin. I hope she didn't feel the way I do today.'

'I'm sure she did,' Esther said as she stemmed a tear, 'but despite her crusty attitude when it came to the career you chose, I always felt that she was secretly very proud of you.'

'And it would be strange if we didn't feel a sense of loss,' Jack observed as the coach turned the corner and disappeared from view. 'But it's made even worse with Bertie being away for the week on what the earl calls "manoeuvres", which so far as I can tell means crawling through undergrowth and pretending to shoot the enemy.'

'Do you think there'll be a war?' Esther asked timidly.

Jack shrugged. 'Who can tell, with the way things are going with our relationship with Germany? But if there is, I think we have to resign ourselves to the fact that Second Lieutenant Enright will be up there in the thick of it. But let's not get all gloomy. On the bright side, we still have Miriam, who's delighted to be moving into the "big girls' room", while Thomas will have more space for his toy trains.' He paused. 'Did Annabelle tell you that Lucy wants her to write a play for her theatre group all about the Suffragettes?'

'At least five times,' Esther said, chuckling, 'while Lily told me how she intends to be the finest nurse that the Nightingale Training School ever produced.'

Jack laughed. 'We'd better go back inside before we catch a chill. These late autumn days can be deceptive.'

'Just another few minutes, while I look all around me, then back at the park, and remind myself of how lucky I am,' Esther said as she snuggled closer to him. 'I was a poor Jewish seamstress living in a single room in an East End lodging house, relying on taking in sewing work, when this dashingly handsome police constable swept me off my feet.'

'As I recall,' Jack replied, 'you were a little reluctant at first, and it was only our joint interest in catching that horrible murderer — each of us for different reasons — that gave us a reason to keep meeting.'

'You can believe that if you like, Jack Enright,' Esther murmured, 'but I'd have found some other reason to keep meeting you, if only by getting myself arrested. Then your mother would have disapproved of me even more.'

'She came to accept you — even love you, in her own stiff way — in the end,' he assured her. 'Not as much as me, of course, which is why we ended up with four children.'

'Don't forget Annabelle,' Esther insisted. 'We have *five* children.'

'Of course we do,' Jack agreed. 'But I hope you aren't tempted to take in any more.'

'No, I think five Enrights are enough to inflict on the world,' Esther said, laughing, 'given the trouble they all seem to attract.'

# A NOTE TO THE READER

Dear Reader,

Thank you for reading this final novel in the Enright series, and I hope that you are as sad to be finally saying goodbye to them as I am.

The extended Enright family have now made it to the height of the Edwardian era, and there were three dominant features of those final years of the reign of Edward VII. The first was the increased demand for Home Rule from those politicians representing Irish constituencies, the second was the growing antipathy between the governments of Britain and Germany, and the third was the growing realisation among women that there was no ongoing justification for their second-rate status in British society. It was this final movement that was most likely to affect the daily lives of our Enright friends, hence my choice to place them in the forefront of the action.

The Women's Social and Political Union (WSPU) had, by the period featured in this novel, come on a long way from its original foundation in 1903. Led by the determined and passionate Emmeline Pankhurst, and her equally strident daughters Christabel and Sylvia, those seeking female suffrage (the equal right of women to both vote, and stand, for Parliament) had progressed beyond polite requests for a condescending audience with the leading politicians of the day, and their agenda had broadened. The demand for the vote was symbolic of a wider demand for equality in all aspects of life, and there was much ground to be covered before that dream could become a reality.

Not only were women effectively banned from any profession in which they might outshine their male counterparts, only able to seek out a livelihood in 'caring' occupations such as nursing, teaching, and domestic management, but they were even subjected to unacceptable treatment within the households of which they were notionally the managers. Domestic violence was so commonplace as to be unremarkable. The authorities were reluctant to intervene, and those who were calling for more rights for women were facing a lengthy uphill battle against the status quo that suited those in control of the nation's affairs.

Little wonder that the Suffragettes, as they became known, grew more militant as the years passed without even an acknowledgement of the need for change, let alone any positive political agenda to bring it about. By 1909, those calling the shots behind the women's front line had ceased making polite requests for an audience, and had established a track record for heckling leading politicians such as the Prime Minister and the Home Secretary during public meetings, for which they were hauled away by police officers, and sentenced to periods of imprisonment for breaches of the peace and other public order offences.

At this point the WSPU severed its official links with the emerging Labour Party, and became more 'middle-class' as it founded its own newspaper, *Votes for Women* — the one that in the pages you have just read gave Annabelle her first openings as what we would today call an 'investigative journalist'. Emmeline Pethick-Lawrence really existed, and along with her husband Frederick published many articles supporting the Suffragette cause, some of them written by Emmeline Pankhurst herself. The following year (1908) the movement adopted the battle colours of purple, white and green, and it was Emmeline Pethick-Lawrence who wrote of them that 'Purple ... stands for the royal blood that flows in the veins of every suffragette... White stands for purity in private and public life... Green is the colour of hope and the emblem of spring.'

This more militant atmosphere, symbolised by the choice of the French Revolutionary rallying song 'La Marseillaise' as their marching melody, led to an increase in physical confrontations with the authorities of the day. This was the point at which I decided to involved the Enrights, beginning with the massive police response in October 1908 to the 'rush' on the House of Commons led by the Pankhursts against a five thousand-strong police defence line that resulted in thirty-seven arrests and ten Suffragette hospitalisations. Realising the need to fight fire with fire, the women formed an army of their own, whom they called 'the Bodyguards', but who became known as 'Amazons'.

I admit to having invented the attack on the Brunner Mond TNT factory in Silvertown by a group of women armed with clubs, so as to give Percy Enright a reason for seeking to infiltrate this group of 'Amazons'. But the authorities were undoubtedly taken aback when they began to receive reports that the women who they had assumed to be weaker than the burly police officers sent in to restrain them were fighting back with weapons concealed under their skirts, or employing unarmed combat techniques that someone had obviously taught them. They became increasingly important to the movement as the level of violence increased.

It is debateable who was responsible for demonstrations moving towards criminal activity, but Ada Wright and Sarah Carwin clearly crossed that line when in June 1909 they threw stones through the windows of the public building in Horse Guards Avenue in the near-riot that was witnessed by

Annabelle and Lily. As recounted in this novel, they reacted to not being afforded the better conditions in Holloway Gaol that they were demanding as 'political prisoners' by smashing their cell windows, then going on hunger strike. Panicking, the prison governor had them released immediately, and Suffragettes who were imprisoned for their beliefs adopted the same tactic. However, the Government reacted with force-feeding, of which Evaline Birkitt became the first victim. The description of her ordeal that I supplied came from an account of force-feeding experienced by Emmeline Pankhurst herself, employing her own words.

Likewise, I quoted, direct from their sources, the arguments for and against force-feeding by the medical fraternity who were consulted once the issue became a political hot potato, and was being commented on by the daily newspapers, of which the *Daily Mail* was one of the most pre-eminent. *The Clarion* also really existed, and was a socialist publication that began to lose circulation after it expressed doubts regarding the methods employed by the Suffragettes to get their message across. The broadsheet *Votes for Women* was the self-pronounced mouthpiece for the WSPU, and the obvious medium to launch Annabelle on her career as a journalist.

'Black Friday' occurred exactly as I described it, with the graphic details Annabelle records being drawn from first-hand accounts written at the time. There would be more incidents to follow, most notably the suicide by Emily Davidson under the hooves of King George V's horse, Anmer, during the running of the 1913 Derby at Epsom. But as the Great War broke out the following year, the women who'd demanded equal rights demonstrated their merits by engaging in 'war work' in the mines, the transport network and even munitions factories in the absence of the men who'd been sent to the trenches. A grateful nation granted women limited voting rights in 1918, completing the process ten years later.

A central theme of this novel — and the inspiration behind its title — was of course what were known as the matrons, employed to guard the interests of female prisoners in police custody. As indicated in the main plot line, the system was inherently flawed because many matrons were connected in some way with the police station to which they were attached. It was too easy for abuses of female prisoners to be either ignored or unreported because the matrons who were supposed to protect them could be persuaded to look the other way, bought off, threatened or even silenced permanently.

In consequence, the statistics for such abuse were unreliable, although many Suffragettes confined within police cells reported to the media that they had been 'rudely handled', as the euphemism went. While there is no evidence that the lady visitors (who I did not invent) were brought in to remedy this flaw in the system, there can be little doubt that these middle-class 'do-gooders', with their Christian values and good intentions, exercised a more restraining influence on what went on behind locked cell doors, although their principal function was to reform female offenders — most notably 'totties' earning a precarious living as street-level sex workers. It was a convenient plot lever to bring Beattie Enright and her Methodist Mission brigade into the fuller picture, and be the means whereby the clandestine activities of Annabelle and Lily were exposed.

A few other elements of the novel are deserving of further clarification, beginning with Percy's old nemesis William Melville. He really existed, and after retiring from Scotland Yard at the rank of Superintendent in charge of the Special Branch established to smoke out Irish terrorists (as we would dub them now), he was recruited to lead what began as MO3, and for some reason was renamed MO5 two years later, masterminding counterintelligence and foreign intelligence operations under the pseudonym 'William Morgan' from covert residential headquarters in London. In an arrangement that predated Fleming's James Bond, and may have inspired it, Melville ended his days as the head of the British Secret Service, employing the codename 'M'.

The explosive potential of trinitrotoluene, or TNT, was first discovered and employed by the Germans in 1902, but the British authorities followed suit almost immediately, combining it with ammonium nitrate in order to fill the shells that were hurled back across the trenches during the Great War. It was partly in these shell-filling factories, risking their lives with every working shift, that the women who'd previously been taking on the authorities as Suffragettes demonstrated their right to constitutional equality with men.

The newspapers referred to in this novel were as depicted, the *Daily Mail* providing a convenient fictional outlet for Annabelle's journalistic talents. As for the medical orderlies into whose ranks Lily was recruited, they really existed, and some of them would later blaze the trail for women in medicine, most notably Dr Elsie Inglis, Dr Louisa Garrett Anderson and Dr Flora Murray, who each founded hospitals providing medical services for soldiers wounded in the Great War. Their pioneering work was of course in the tradition of Florence Nightingale, who died aged ninety in August 1910, and whose Nightingale Training School in St Thomas's Hospital was about to welcome Lily Enright into its ranks.

I did not invent either the lady who provided Lily with that opportunity, or her influential husband. 'Galloper' Jack Seely was a hero of the Second Boer War who became Baron

Mottistone, MP for Bromley (whose constituency included the Nightingale family home), Under-Secretary of State for the Colonies in the Asquith Government, a Privy Councillor and a lifelong friend of Winston Churchill. His first wife, who was still alive in 1910, was named Emily, and he was succeeded by eight children, one of whom might conceivably have been the little girl named Emily whom Lily brought back from the dead. This scene involved a little literary licence on my part, and I hope I have not offended any Seely descendants.

The test case of *Leigh v Gladstone* brought back memories of my days as a Law student, and may still be found quoted in some legal textbooks regarding the right of those in authority to intervene to preserve the lives of those for whom they are responsible, whether they like it or not. Finally, Selfridge's department store in Oxford Street, which inspired such wonderment in Annabelle and Lily, was, in 1909, newly opened, and the last word in retail luxury. The groundbreaking facilities were masterminded by its American founder Harry Selfridge, setting a new high bar for retail emporia.

As ever, I would be delighted to see a review of my book posted on **Amazon** or **Goodreads**. Alternatively, feel free to visit and contact me via my author website: **davidfieldauthor.com**.

Happy reading!

David

SAPERE
BOOKS

www.ingramcontent.com/pod-product-compliance
Lightning Source LLC
LaVergne TN
LVHW091145080826
845145LV00008B/2265

* 9 7 8 0 8 5 4 9 5 8 6 2 7 *